LOVE AND A CHEETAH

Barbara Cartland

Barbara Cartland Ebooks Ltd

This edition © 2020

ISBNs

9781788672498   EPUB

9781788672504   PAPERBACK

Book design by M-Y Books
m-ybooks.co.uk

THE BARBARA CARTLAND ETERNAL COLLECTION

The Barbara Cartland Eternal Collection is the unique opportunity to collect all five hundred of the timeless beautiful romantic novels written by the world's most celebrated and enduring romantic author.

Named the Eternal Collection because Barbara's inspiring stories of pure love, just the same as love itself, the books will be published on the internet at the rate of four titles per month until all five hundred are available.

The Eternal Collection, classic pure romance available worldwide for all time .

THE LATE DAME BARBARA CARTLAND

Barbara Cartland, who sadly died in May 2000 at the grand age of ninety eight, remains one of the world's most famous romantic novelists. With worldwide sales of over one billion, her outstanding 723 books have been translated into thirty six different languages, to be enjoyed by readers of romance globally.

Writing her first book 'Jigsaw' at the age of 21, Barbara became an immediate bestseller. Building upon this initial success, she wrote continuously throughout her life, producing bestsellers for an astonishing 76 years. In addition to Barbara Cartland's legion of fans in the UK and across Europe, her books have always been immensely popular in the USA. In 1976 she achieved the unprecedented feat of having books at numbers 1 & 2 in the prestigious B. Dalton Bookseller bestsellers list.

Although she is often referred to as the 'Queen of Romance', Barbara Cartland also wrote several historical biographies, six autobiographies and numerous theatrical plays as well as books on life, love, health and cookery. Becoming one of Britain's most popular media personalities and dressed in her trademark pink, Barbara spoke on radio and television about social and political issues, as well as making many public appearances.

In 1991 she became a Dame of the Order of the British Empire for her contribution to literature and her work for humanitarian and charitable causes.

Known for her glamour, style, and vitality Barbara Cartland became a legend in her own lifetime. Best remembered for her wonderful romantic novels and loved by millions of readers worldwide, her books remain treasured for their heroic heroes, plucky heroines and traditional values. But above all, it was Barbara Cartland's overriding belief in the positive power of love to help, heal and improve the quality of life for everyone that made her truly unique.

AUTHOR'S NOTE

George Stubbs was one of the greatest of English painters.

For some time he was underrated by being labelled 'Mr. Stubbs, the Horse Painter'.

Gradually, however, people began to realise how important he was and he then achieved equal recognition with his contemporaries, Reynolds and Gainsborough, in the foremost rank of British Art.

No one but Stubbs could produce such originality in his paintings of animals and he also had a similar genius in his portraiture of human beings.

Sportsmen have collected Stubbs ever since he first started to paint horses. The Queen and other members of the Royal Family have his paintings in their collections.

The cheetah, which Stubbs portrayed so brilliantly in one of his pictures, is the fastest mammal in the world over a short distance.

The name 'cheetah' originated in India and means 'the spotted one'.

In history the cheetah was used as an emblem on the reliefs and friezes of the Ancient Egyptians where they exemplified courage and speed.

There are records of the cheetah being a Royal pet of Genghis Khan and the Emperor Charlemagne.

For many years Indian Princes used to hunt with them, training them to run up game for them, but since 1930 there is no record of a cheetah living wild in India and they now exist only in parts of Africa.

The cheetah purrs like a cat when he is pleased and happy, his whole body vibrating like a motor car engine.

They will lick the face of anyone they particularly like, but to nibble someone's ear is a sign of great affection.

A recent census has discovered that, while the cheetah is still to be found, they will only survive if they are protected.

CHAPTER ONE
1878

Ilesa finished arranging the flowers in the Church and, standing at the Church door to admire her work, she thought that they looked very lovely.

It had been a joy to have so many looking colourful and happy now that it was May.

There were not only the usual bright spring flowers but also those that bloomed at the beginning of the summer.

She took a last look round the little Norman Church where she had been baptised by her father and confirmed when she was twelve year's old.

She then walked towards the West door.

There she stopped to look back again and admire the Altar covered with Arum lilies that had come from the garden.

There were also a dozen or more golden azaleas and she knew that the one person who would have appreciated them more than anyone else would have been her mother.

She could never remember a time when every room in the Vicarage had not been filled with flowers.

Because the people in the village had loved her mother, they had always brought her the first flowers that came out in their small but well-kept gardens.

Closing the Church door behind her, Ilesa walked from the porch down past the ancient tombstones that were almost swallowed up by wreaths of moss.

Beyond these was the lych-gate that led into the Park.

And far away in the distance she could see a glimpse of Harlestone Hall where her father had been born and brought up.

The sixth Earl of Harlestone, as regards his three sons, had kept firmly to established English tradition.

Robert, his eldest son, who would inherit the title on his death, had taken a Commission in the family Regiment,

Henry, his second son, had entered the Royal Navy as a Midshipman and had risen by sheer merit to gain command of a Destroyer, a new addition to the British fleet.

Mark, his third son, following tradition went into the Church and was offered the choice of any of the Livings on the Harlestone Estate.

The Honourable Mark Harle had accepted the situation because it was what he had been brought up to expect.

He had also unfortunately accepted his father's decision as to whom he should marry and the Earl had chosen for his eldest son the daughter of a celebrated Peer, who had money and assets of her own.

His second son had totally refused to be hurried up the aisle and had managed to remain unmarried. He, however, lost his life in a battle at sea when his Destroyer was sunk.

Mark had married when he was only twenty-two and his bride was the daughter of a gentleman who found Harlestone Hall and the Earl himself somewhat imposing. The young couple had nothing in common and had been unhappy from the very start.

Although no one said so openly, it had been a relief when after six years of arguing and wrangling with each other, she had, in one exceptionally cold winter, contracted pneumonia from which she did not recover.

She had left behind a daughter aged five who had grown up to be very like her mother.

Once Mark was free and the prescribed year of mourning had ended, he had wasted no time.

He was now the Vicar of Littlestone and he married the girl who he had always loved, but had been too shy to approach.

She was the daughter of a neighbouring Country Squire and they had met at a party given by her parents.

Elizabeth was so beautiful that he had been convinced that she would never look in his direction.

However she had in fact loved him ever since she had been a child.

Elizabeth had managed to remain unmarried and her parents were too fond of their daughter to force her into doing anything against her inclinations.

Elizabeth and Mark were married quietly in the country and after an ecstatic honeymoon they had settled down in Littlestone to make the village a happy place.

Their daughter, Ilesa, was born a year after they were married and the only sadness in their lives was that Elizabeth could have no more children.

They, however, found Ilesa enchanting.

All through her childhood she could not remember a time when the Vicarage was not filled with love and happiness.

It was only as her half-sister, Doreen, grew older that there was anything to disturb the calm serene atmosphere.

Being like her mother, Doreen had always wanted things that she could not have, such as Parisian dresses, a stately home and endless jewels.

It was a relief therefore when her grandfather, the Earl, insisted on her going to a smart Seminary for Young Ladies in London.

She then went to what was known as a 'Finishing School' in Florence.

And the two schools certainly changed Doreen's life.

She had always found the Vicarage confining and she was not interested in the lives of the villagers or in anything that concerned her father's vocation.

While the old Earl was alive, she spent most of her time at Harlestone Hall.

She loved the big rooms and high ceilings and, whenever possible, she slept in one of the State bedrooms with its huge four-poster bed.

"I do like grandeur!" she said to her small half-sister, who did not understand what she was talking about.

Finally, when she was seventeen, Doreen had 'come out' in London as a *debutante*.

She was presented at Buckingham Palace to Her Majesty Queen Victoria by one of the Earl's sisters, who had no daughters of her own.

At the end of her first Season Doreen had married Lord Barker and it was considered an excellent match at the time despite the fact that he was very much older than she was.

From that moment, her father, stepmother and half-sister saw very little of her.

They did not miss her for the simple reason that she had always been somehow out of place in the Vicarage of Littlestone.

Elizabeth Harle had tried in every way to be a mother to her stepdaughter, but she knew privately that it was the one big failure in her life.

When two years ago she had died, Doreen had not even come back to Harlestone Hall for the funeral.

She did, however, send an enormous if somewhat flamboyant wreath of spring flowers.

It looked incongruous among the smaller but loving tributes that had been sent by the local villagers.

There were little bunches of wild flowers from the village children, which Ilesa found very touching.

Because they all knew how much Elizabeth Harle had loved flowers, the whole of the neighbourhood had contributed. They stripped their gardens of every leaf and blossom as a profound tribute to her and her memory.

To Mark Harle it was a dreadful blow that left him dazed and he found it hard to believe that he had lost someone who he had loved so dearly.

Ilesa understood, but there was little that she could do to comfort him. She only tried in every way that she could think of to take her mother's place.

She arranged the flowers in the Church, she visited the sick in the village and comforted the bereaved.

She also tried to find employment for the local youngsters when they left school.

It had, the year before, come as a disaster to the whole village when the new Earl of Harlestone had closed the Big House.

It was not unreasonable because Robert had been recently appointed Governor of the North-West Frontier Province in India and this meant that he would be living in India for the next five years.

"It's no use, Mark," he had said to his brother, "I cannot afford to keep up the house as well as meet my expenses in India, which will undoubtedly be very heavy."

"What is to happen to the people who have always worked in The Hall?" Mark Harle had asked him. "Some of them have worked for us loyally and diligently for over thirty years and in one or two cases even longer."

"I know, I know," his brother Robert replied testily. "But I just cannot find the money anywhere!"

The two brothers had sat up talking all night.

Finally, on the Vicar's insistence, the Earl had agreed to retain four of the oldest servants to act as caretakers.

Watkins, the Head Gardener and then Oakes, the Head Gamekeeper, were to keep their cottages.

"I am sure I can find local work for them to do," the Vicar offered, "and I will help with their pensions, which will at least keep them from starving."

"You know you cannot afford to do that!" Robert protested. "The best thing we can do is to sell something."

His brother looked at him in consternation.

"Sell?" he enquired. "But everything in the house is entailed onto future generations of the family."

"There must be a few things that are not," Robert argued, "and there are some outlying plots of land that could be disposed of, even though we will not be paid much for them."

Finally, one way and another, the Earl found the means to allow Watkins and Oakes enough to live on.

The Vicar encouraged the gardener to grow fruit and vegetables that could be sold in the local market.

Oakes was to keep down the vermin and sell what rabbits, pigeons and ducks he could shoot or trap.

"It will not bring in much," Mark confided to his brother, "but perhaps enough even to pay a youth to help them. At least it will keep them busy."

He gave a deep sigh as he added,

"I just don't know what the village is going to do. As you well know, Robert, the great ambition of all the young people has always been to be taken on at the Big House."

"I know, I know!" Robert agreed. "But I can hardly refuse to become Governor of the North-West Frontier Province, which is a great honour, simply because the village wants me to stay in England!"

What he said was meant to be a joke, but there was still a bitter note in his voice.

"The real trouble," Mark said soothingly, "is that the Harles have never been rich and Papa was extravagant, especially where horses were concerned."

"That is true," Robert nodded, "and I suggest that you have the choice of two horses that you most want and I will sell the rest."

"Must you really sell them?" the Vicar asked. "It seems a pity when there is such a very fine collection in the stables at the moment."

"I know, but I can hardly take them to India with me and they will be a bit long in the teeth when I come back."

Finally the Vicar took four of the horses and the rest were sold mostly to locals.

Ilesa cried when she saw them being taken away. She had always been allowed to ride any horses she liked in her grandfather's stables.

She had grown to greatly love the animals and there was nothing that she could not do with them.

"Miss Ilesa's got a right way with 'orses," the grooms would say.

She was allowed to mount the most obstreperous stallions and even those that were not fully broken.

She well knew that she had as they said, 'a way with' the animals and the horses would always obey her even though some of the stable lads were too nervous to mount them.

The only good thing about closing up Harlestone Hall was that at least it was not leased to a stranger.

"If I was not still able to ride in the Park, swim in the lake and read the books in the library," Ilesa said to her father, "I would cry my eyes out!"

"I know that, my dearest," the Vicar replied, "and that is why we must be very grateful that, if it is closed to everybody else, it is open to us."

There was no doubt, however, that, as the years passed, they began to take their toll on the building.

The wooden doors and window frames needed repainting and the garden, with no one to tend it, began to look just like a hayfield.

The flowerbeds were disappearing amongst the weeds and Ilesa had to fight her way through banks of nettles to pick the flowers that still stubbornly managed to push their way through them.

Two of the green houses were in danger of falling in and there did not seem to be any point in urging her father to have them repaired.

"Your uncle will be in India for at least another two years," he would tell her.

Ilesa still went to the library to take out the books that she wanted to read.

She would look at the pictures hanging on the walls and think how wonderful they would be if they were re-framed or at least dusted.

The furniture wanted polishing, so did the fireplaces and the fireguard, as they had been before her grandfather had died.

One of the things, however, that delighted Ilesa was that he had left her father two of his pictures in his will.

These were not entailed for he had been given them by his Godfather.

They were two pictures by George Stubbs, the celebrated and popular painter of horses, who was commissioned by the aristocracy to paint their best racehorses.

As the Vicar pointed out, the two pictures had been cleverly framed to show the subject off to its best advantage.

"They are lovely, Papa," Ilesa exclaimed over and over again. "I am sure that Grandpapa knew that you would appreciate them more than anyone else."

"I am delighted to have them," the Vicar beamed, "and I am also exceedingly grateful to my father for leaving me a little money that I can spend on those really in need."

Ilesa repressed an impulse to say that she was really in need of a new gown.

But she understood that her father was thinking about those who could not find local employment now that the Big House was closed up.

There were also the elderly and they could no longer turn to his Lordship when their cottages needed repairing or they themselves were desperately in need of help through illness or having to eat substandard food.

Because he could never say 'no' to anyone in need, the Vicar took on an extra groom to look after the horses as well as a boy he did not really need to work in the garden.

Mrs. Briggs, who had been at the Vicarage ever since Ilesa could remember, had enough help in the kitchen.

Nanny, who took over the running of the house very competently after Elizabeth Harle's death had

had a young girl thrust upon her and she proved to be more trouble than she was worth.

Nevertheless, if it was what the Master wanted, they accepted it all with a good grace.

Walking back to the Vicarage after leaving the Church, Ilesa was thinking of her father's concern for two of the villagers who were seriously ill.

She was also planning to surprise him on his birthday, which was the following week.

She had learned that a book had recently been published in London that contained many illustrations of pictures by George Stubbs and she just knew that it would delight him to read it and he would enjoy learning more about the famous artist whose pictures now adorned his study walls.

She decided that she would write to Hatchards, the well-known London bookshop that was patronised by the Social world, and have the book sent to her.

She would then give it to him on his birthday together with a number of other smaller presents that she had been collecting for him.

All of which she would wrap up and tie with pink ribbon which was a custom that her mother had inaugurated not only at Christmastime but for birthdays as well.

"Everybody likes presents," her mother had declared, "and the more the merrier!"

She had always contrived to have at least half-a-dozen presents for Ilesa on her birthday and the same number or even more for her husband.

They ranged from one large fairly expensive present to something small and amusing. A jar of the special mustard he preferred to any others, a comb of the best local honey or a handkerchief embroidered with his initials.

Every present was a surprise and therefore fun to open.

Ilesa was seriously determined that her father should have the largest number of presents possible this year.

As she then turned into the Vicarage drive, she stared in astonishment at a smart carriage drawn by two well-matched horses that was standing outside the front door.

She was certain as she drew nearer that the carriage was not one that belonged to any of their neighbours.

'Who can it possibly be?' she wondered.

She then tried to remember if her father was at home today and then she recalled that he had driven off early that morning to visit the two ill parishioners.

He was then going to visit a farmer on the outskirts of the Harlestone Estate whose wife was expecting a baby in two months' time.

"I hope to be back for luncheon," he had said to Ilesa before he left, "but if I am late, don't wait for me. You know how long-winded Farmer Johnson can be!"

Ilesa had laughed.

She knew that because her father was so sympathetic and understanding people were inclined to talk to him for far too long and so use up his time which could be better spent elsewhere.

He knew, however, that 'getting it off their chests', as he frequently called it, was often a great help.

He was therefore patient and stayed when he visited people for much longer than he had intended, listening to all sorts of tales of woe and obscure ailments.

'I wonder who it is who wants him?' Ilesa puzzled.

She reached the front door and took another quick look at the two horses that were drawing the carriage

They were certainly outstanding stallions, but she did not recognise the livery that the coachman on the box was wearing.

The front door was open and she walked up the steps and inside.

She entered the drawing room, which was on the other side of the house looking onto the garden.

Standing by the window she saw a slender figure and it was most certainly someone very smart, wearing a hat with long feathers and an elegant bustle.

As she hesitated in the doorway, the woman turned round.

Ilesa gave a cry of pleasure.

"Doreen! I did not expect you! Where have you come from?"

She ran across the room to kiss her half-sister.

Doreen accepted the embrace, but made no attempt to return it.

"I found the house empty," she began. "Where were you?"

"I was arranging the flowers in the Church," Ilesa explained. "You know it is Saturday today."

Doreen gave a little laugh that had no humour in it.

"Of course it never occurred to me for a moment and you certainly look somewhat untidy."

Ilesa pulled off her hat.

"I know," she admitted. "I went up to The Hall to pick some of the flowers there, but the place is so overgrown that it's virtually impossible not to be almost torn to bits by bushes of brambles."

"It's ridiculous to let it go to rack and ruin," Doreen pointed out sharply.

Ilesa knew that it would be useless to try to explain to her that their uncle could not afford to do anything else.

Instead she said,

"It's lovely to see you. Can I fetch you a cup of coffee? Are you staying for luncheon with us today?"

"I suppose so if there is anything to eat!" Doreen replied somewhat sarcastically.

"Of course there is," Ilesa answered, "and Mrs. Briggs will certainly do her best if she knows you are here."

"Good Heavens! Is that old woman still with you?" Doreen exclaimed.

"She looks older than she really is," Ilesa said quickly, "and we could not do without her. You know that she has been with us ever since we were children."

Doreen's mind was obviously on something different.

And after a moment she suggested,

"Well, go and tell Mrs. Briggs that I shall be here for luncheon. Then I want to talk to you."

"What about your coachman?" Ilesa asked her.

Doreen hesitated for a moment.

Then she said,

"He can eat here if you can feed him. If not, he will have to go to the nearest inn."

"Of course he must have something to eat here," Ilesa murmured.

She ran from the room.

In the kitchen Mrs. Briggs was kneading a basinful of dough for their pudding tomorrow.

They always had a pie on Sunday because it was the Vicar's favourite.

"Mrs. Briggs," Ilesa said, raising her voice because the old woman was growing deaf, "Miss Doreen is here and is staying for luncheon."

"'Er Ladyship?" Mrs. Briggs exclaimed. "God bless my soul! She's not been 'ere for nigh on three years!"

"I know," Ilesa replied, "but she is here now and her coachman would like something to eat too. I am sure you can manage it."

"Aye, I can manage right enough," Mrs. Briggs agreed, "and it's lucky it be that I bought that leg of lamb for luncheon today. It was to 'ave lasted most of the week, but not with two extras gnawin' away at it!"

Mrs. Briggs was talking more to herself than to Ilesa, who left the kitchen to hurry back to the drawing room.

On the way she did her best to tidy her hair and straiten her old muslin dress as she knew that she must look a mess compared to Doreen in her impeccable outfit.

Ilesa was wishing that she had had time to put on one of her better gowns before her sister had arrived.

And then she told herself philosophically that nothing she possessed could compare with what Doreen was wearing.

Doreen was now exceedingly rich since her elderly husband had died from a heart attack three years ago and she had only come home to see her family once and that was shortly after her bereavement.

Occasionally Ilesa and her father had heard of what a success she was being in London and they read in the social columns of the newspapers of parties she gave that were attended by all the most important people in the Social world.

Their neighbours always talked enthusiastically about Doreen whenever Ilesa and her father visited them.

"Your sister is one of the most beautiful women in London!" Ilesa had been told a hundred times. "I have heard that she is constantly at Marlborough House being entertained by the Prince of Wales in great style."

Although she lived in the country, Ilesa was well aware of what the ambition of every woman was. It was to be invited by the Prince of Wales and his beautiful Danish wife, Princess Alexandra.

'The Marlborough House Set was whispered about, gossiped about and was an inevitable part of every conversation and Ilesa felt sometimes that she could write a book on all that she had heard about it.

She was, however, not particularly interested and recognised that she was never likely to be invited to Marlborough House.

Her half-sister had never once asked her to stay with her in London at her smart and beautiful apartment in Half Moon Street.

Now, astoundingly, she had appeared at their house without any warning at all.

Ilesa was wise enough to realise that there would be some ulterior motive for Doreen's coming home all of a sudden.

It was such a strange thing for her to do that for a moment Ilesa had been afraid that some tragedy had occurred that could bring anguish to the family.

Doreen, however, certainly looked as if nothing on earth could perturb her in any way.

Ilesa did not miss the diamond and pearl earrings and the three strands of pearls at her throat and there was a diamond brooch in the shape of a colourful butterfly on the shoulder of her gown.

She could not help thinking that just one of Doreen's jewels could support a dozen families in the village for many years and it would undoubtedly make her father very happy.

And then she told herself that her always vivid imagination was clearly running away with her.

Doreen only ever communicated with her father and herself at Christmas and completely ignored their birthdays and Ilesa had been concerned that her father would feel hurt.

Then she thought it all over very carefully.

From the moment Doreen had been sent to an elite school and then on to Florence, she had made it more or less obvious that she despised her family and would have as little to do with them as she could possibly get away with.

She had intimated that she wished to live a very different sort of life.

It was certainly what she had achieved with Lord Barker and only occasionally did Ilesa think it unkind.

Now that Doreen was a rich widow, she would not want to spend time with her relatives in the country.

'I cannot think why she is here now!' Ilesa thought as she walked into the drawing room.

While she had been away talking to Mrs. Briggs, Doreen had made herself comfortable. She had taken off her feathered hat and was lying back languidly in an armchair with her feet on a footstool.

As Ilesa reached her, she ordered Ilesa,

"Now sit down and listen to what I have to tell you. You have to help me because there is no one else I can trust."

"Are you in – some sort of trouble, Doreen?" Ilesa enquired a little timidly.

"Of course I am!" Doreen snapped. "Otherwise I would not be here."

"I am so sorry to hear it," Ilesa said gently, "and, of course, Papa and I will help you if it is at all possible."

As she spoke, she could not imagine how either of them could possibly help Doreen in any way.

She could not be needing money of that Ilesa was certain.

Because it seemed friendlier, she knelt down at her sister's feet and looked up at her.

"Now tell me, Doreen," she asked softly, "what is worrying you?"

Doreen gave a sigh that was really more one of exasperation than of distress.

"You have to help me simply because there is no one else who can and what I want, needless to say, is very very important to me."

"What do you want?" Ilesa asked curiously.

"To put it bluntly," Doreen replied, "I want to marry the Duke of Mountheron."

Ilesa gave a little gasp.

"The Duke of Mountheron? But – does he want to – marry you?"

The questions seemed to tumble out of her mouth simply because she was so surprised by Doreen unlikely revelation.

She had naturally somehow expected that sooner or later Doreen would marry again and she felt sure that it would be to someone just as significant as Lord Barker had been and a brilliant match.

But even that was hardly on the same level as marrying a Duke!

As it so happened, Ilesa had heard of the Duke of Mountheron because he owned some successful racehorses.

Her father, who was an exceptionally good rider, took *The Racing Times* every week.

It always carried graphic descriptions of the horses that were running in every race that week and went into considerable details regarding their breeding and there were also articles about their owners.

The Duke of Mountheron had won the Derby last year and his horse had come in second the year before.

He had in the last few years won nearly all the Classic races at Ascot and Newmarket.

Ilesa and her father had often discussed his stable and had decided that the Duke was undoubtedly the finest racehorse owner in the whole country.

"I have heard that he has recently bought some mares from Syria," the Vicar said, "or it might have been his brother. Anyway the horses have an Arab strain in them that makes them exceptional at the Racecourse."

"I would love to see them," Ilesa had exclaimed.

"So would I," the Vicar smiled, "and if there is any chance of his having runners in any of the races near here, then, of course, we must try to attend the meeting."

He gave a sigh.

"Unfortunately Newmarket is too long a journey and we would have to stay the night which would be expensive."

"If we left very early, I daresay we could find our way back if there was a moon," Ilesa suggested.

The Vicar smiled.

"That is an idea and we will certainly think about it. In the meantime we have to decide which horses we are going to ride in the Point-to-Point next week. I am also hoping that Red Rufus will be strong enough for me to hunt with him next autumn."

Red Rufus had hurt one of his legs jumping a high hedge and Ilesa was tending it with her usual tender loving care.

She had bandaged his leg and massaged it each day and the groom who looked after the horses was quite certain that she prayed every night on her knees for Red Rufus to get well and become robust again.

Now she declared,

"I can assure you that Red Rufus will be perfectly well in a month's time. He will have to be ridden carefully and slowly at first, but I am certain that he will be well enough to hunt for you in the autumn, Papa."

The Vicar patted her arm.

"That is what I want to do and I know, my dearest child, that it is all due to you that he is not completely crippled."

He smiled again.

"In Medieval times you would have surely been burned as a witch, so just be careful!"

"If I am a witch, then I am like Mama, who was a white one," Ilesa replied. "You know that is what they used to say about her in the village. They never sent for the doctor, but always for Mama. Her herbs healed them far quicker than anything that the doctor could have prescribed."

"That is true," the Vicar agreed, "and, when I had a headache, she used to massage my forehead and it always disappeared immediately."

Ilesa did not answer.

The pain in her father's voice when he spoke of his beloved wife who he had loved so deeply and lost was very poignant.

She knew that there was nothing she could say or do to comfort him.

Now she looked at her half-sister in some surprise.

It flashed through her mind that only her mother would have been able to cope with a difficult situation like Doreen wanting to marry a Duke.

There was a little pause as she cleared her throat.

And then Doreen asserted strongly,

"I *must* marry him! I *will* marry him! I am *determined* to marry him! But at this moment only you and Papa can help me."

CHAPTER TWO

Ilesa was just going to answer when there was a barking and scratching at the door.

She jumped up.

"It's the dogs," she said unnecessarily. "They have been shut up all the time that I was in the Church. Now they know I am back."

"Don't let them come anywhere near me!" Doreen shouted out. "They will leave hairs on my skirt."

Ilesa was not listening to her.

She hurried across the room to open the door and then the dogs burst in, jumping and barking with delight at seeing her.

They were two cocker spaniels and they always went everywhere with her. Ilesa loved them as much as they loved her.

If she was away, even for an hour or so, they behaved as if she had come back from a long voyage.

She now patted them lovingly and calmed them down.

Then she sat down again on the floor beside her sister.

"I am sorry, Doreen. I know that you dislike dogs, but they will be no trouble now."

The dogs had settled down quietly near to Ilesa and were no longer making a noise.

Doreen did not speak and after a moment Ilesa said gently,

"You were saying that you needed us to help you."

She heard her sister take a deep breath before she began,

"I met the Duke just two months ago and I knew at once that he was bowled over by my beauty."

There was a note of distinct satisfaction in her voice that Ilesa did not miss.

"He is, of course, very sought after in London," Doreen went on, "and that he attaches himself to me at parties and that the hostesses seat us next to each other at dinners is most flattering for me."

"I can understand his being bowled over by your beauty," Ilesa commented. "You are much more beautiful now than you have ever been, Doreen."

"I realise that," her sister replied, "but, as you well know, I am now nearly twenty-six and I want to be married again."

"I am sure lots of men have already asked you to be their wife," Ilesa pointed out loyally.

"That is true," Doreen agreed. "At the same time the Duke of Mountheron is unique and, as I have already said, I intend to marry him."

There was a pause in the conversation.

Then Ilesa said, almost as if she was speaking to herself,

"But he has not yet – asked you?"

"He has been very close to doing so," Doreen replied. "In fact the last time we were together, I felt instinctively that the words were trembling on his lips."

She gave a little sigh and Ilesa asked,

"Then what – happened?"

"That is what I am going to tell you," Doreen went on in a different voice. "The Duke had to leave London for a short time and, because I was feeling lonely, I went out with Lord Randall, who fell in love with me more than two years ago."

Ilesa was listening to her sister attentively, realising that somebody else had now come on the scene.

"He persuaded me against my better judgement," Doreen continued, "to stay with him last night at a hotel called *The Three Feathers*, which is about ten miles from here."

Ilesa stared at her sister in amazement.

"Stay – with you?" she questioned. "Alone?"

"Oh, don't be so ridiculous, Ilesa!" Doreen said crossly. "You may live here among the turnips and cabbages, but you must be aware that in London every pretty married woman has *affaires de coeur*. As I have already told you, Hugo Randall has been in love with me for some time."

"But – you are in – love with the Duke!"

Ilesa was so surprised and shocked that she found the words difficult to utter and they were almost incoherent.

There was a little pause before Doreen answered her,

"I intend to *marry* the Duke, which is a very different thing."

Ilesa felt bewildered.

She had vaguely known, as Doreen had said, that people in London, especially those in the Marlborough House Set, had wildly promiscuous love affairs.

These were talked about *sotto voce* by some of the people at parties she had attended with her father and mother, but somehow she had never thought of any of her own friends or certainly not her relations being so involved.

It was an incredible shock to learn that her sister, who was in love with one man, should have an *affaire de coeur* with another.

She could not understand it and she could not accept it as something ever happening in her own experience.

Her father and mother had been so completely devoted to each other and they had never discussed or gossiped about such matters.

"What happened," Doreen was saying, "and you can hardly believe that I could have such bad luck, was that at dawn this morning when I was still asleep, a man whom I know and whose name is Sir Mortimer Jackson, burst into my bedroom!"

She paused for a moment as if to make the story even more dramatic.

"'The hotel is on fire!' he shouted out. 'Get up quickly or you will be burnt to death'!"

Ilesa gave a little cry of horror.

"The hotel was on fire, Doreen? How terrible! How did you escape?"

"As it turned out, it was a false alarm," Doreen replied, "but, of course, I was extremely frightened."

"Naturally," Ilesa murmured.

"Hugo Randall got up – " Doreen continued.

"From – your – bed?" Ilesa stammered.

"Yes, yes, from my bed!" Doreen answered testily. "He would have gone back to his own room in just a few minutes. That is why it was such bad luck for me that the ghastly Sir Mortimer should burst in on us!"

She spoke very angrily and there was a frown between her beautiful eyes.

"And you – say there was – not really – a fire?" Ilesa murmured.

"Hugo Randall went to see what all the fuss was about and found that one of the servants had upset some hot fat or something combustible on the stove."

Doreen's voice was seething as she continued,

"It caused a dense cloud of smoke to rise up past Sir Mortimer's window. I always thought that he was a stupid idiotic man, but unfortunately he is also dangerous."

"You – mean," Ilesa queried her, trying to understand the extraordinary scenario, "he recognised you."

"Of course he did and, because I have always disliked him and made my feelings very clear, he will undoubtedly tell the Duke in graphic detail all that he saw this morning."

At last Ilesa grasped the problem and why Doreen was plainly so upset.

If the Duke learned of the way she had behaved with Lord Randall, he was not likely to ask her to become his wife.

She looked at her sister helplessly, thinking how could she possibly help her to find a way out of such a predicament?

"I have thought it out carefully," Doreen now said in a practical manner. "What I have to do is to make the Duke propose to me before he returns to London where Sir Mortimer will be waiting for him."

"Are you – are you quite – certain that is – what he will do?" Ilesa asked. "It sounds very ungentlemanly. Papa has always said – that a gentleman never mentions a woman's name – disparagingly in public – or he would be thrown out of his Clubs."

"Men like Sir Mortimer do *not* behave like gentlemen!" Doreen said scathingly. "He ingratiates himself with the Nobility by giving them information that they find amusing or else in some way helpful."

"Then how can you prevent him from telling the Duke about you?" Ilesa asked.

"I am making sure," Doreen replied, "as I have just said, that I see the Duke first. That is why I sent a note immediately by my footman asking him to come here this afternoon."

Ilesa stared at her in sheer astonishment.

"To come here?" she repeated, "but why? And how? Where is he?"

Doreen was about to answer her questions.

And then she gave an exclamation.

"The servants!" she cried. "I never thought of the servants."

She jumped abruptly out of the chair where she had been sitting and Ilesa then heard her running across the hall towards the front door.

She supposed that Mrs. Briggs would not invite the coachman in for his luncheon until it was ready. He would therefore be with the carriage outside waiting for his instructions.

She could hear Doreen's voice in the distance although she could not hear what she was saying.

There came the sound of rolling wheels and she reckoned that Doreen's carriage was being turned round.

She did not move, but one of the spaniels curled up beside her and she stroked the soft fur of its head.

She found it hard to believe what her sister had told her and even harder to understand her reprehensible behaviour.

How was it possible that Doreen could go to an inn and share a bed with a man who she was not married to?

Ilesa had never been to *The Three Feathers*, but she had heard that it was thought to be the best inn in the County.

In fact it was used by gentlemen from London when they took part in the local Point-to-Points and Steeplechases.

Vaguely at the back of her mind she remembered her grandfather recommending friends to stay there for the Hunt Ball or some other important function when The Hall would be full.

People from London then had to be accommodated wherever they could find a bed in the locality.

But Ilesa had never imagined that her own sister would stay there much less behave in a way that would have completely horrified her mother and would deeply distress her father.

Doreen then came back into the room.

"It slipped my mind," she said as she walked back to the chair that she had been sitting on, "that if the Duke comes here, his servants will talk to my coachman. And he might tell them where I was staying last night."

"But – but how do – you know that the Duke – will come here?" Ilesa asked her.

"I remembered," Doreen explained, "that Papa has those two pictures by Stubbs, which you both made such a fuss about."

Ilesa looked at her sister questioningly and Doreen went on,

"The Duke himself owns a very special collection of Stubbs's pictures and they are all kept at his country house."

She gave a little sigh of satisfaction.

"It suddenly occurred to me that, as he was staying in the neighbourhood, he would be thrilled to see

Papa's pictures and, of course, I shall be here waiting for him."

"You say he is in the neighbourhood?" Ilesa asked. "Where is he staying?"

"With the Lord Lieutenant, of course, the Marquis of Exford!"

Doreen spoke as if her sister had asked her a particularly silly question and Ilesa knew that she was right.

Of course the Duke of Mountheron would be staying with the Marquis of Exford.

He was a very distinguished man with a notably fine stable. His house was some distance from Littlestone, but the Vicar and his wife had often been invited to dine.

They also went to the Garden Party that the Marquis and his wife gave every year for all the most distinguished ladies and gentlemen of the County.

"If the Duke is staying with the Lord Lieutenant," Ilesa said reflectively, "do you really think that he will come here because you have asked him to?"

"I have told you, it is only a question of time before he asks me to marry him," Doreen snapped, "and I cannot risk losing everything by letting that rat Sir Mortimer blacken my character!"

Ilesa thought for a moment.

Then she quizzed her sister,

"What will you do if he informs the Duke after he has proposed to you?"

"That is where you have to help me," Doreen answered. "I stayed here last night. In fact I have been here ever since the Duke left London, which was two days ago."

Ilesa stared at her sister.

"You mean – you are going to – tell him a – complete lie?"

"Of course," Doreen admitted, "and you are going to substantiate it and make it very clear that I have been staying in my old home for a while, enjoying myself by being with you and Papa."

Ilesa drew in her breath.

"You know that – Papa will not – lie," she said quickly.

"Then we will talk to him about it very carefully and you must say to the Duke, 'it has been lovely to have Doreen here at the Vicarage with us these last few days'."

It was with difficulty that Ilesa did not reply that she too disliked telling lies under any circumstances.

Her father and mother had been very insistent that she should always in her life tell the truth, the whole truth and nothing but the truth.

Yet she knew now that she had to do what Doreen wished.

Otherwise her sister would go into one of her tantrums, which had always frightened her when she was a child.

Because she was so much younger and smaller, Doreen had bullied her and she had made Ilesa do what she wanted even if it meant pulling her hair or slapping her face.

Ilesa doubted if she would use actual violence, but she was well aware of what a scene there would be if she told Doreen that she would not support her in telling shameless lies.

Doreen characteristically assumed that Ilesa had immediately acquiesced in doing as she wanted.

"Now we have not much time," she said briskly, "so you had better go and tidy yourself. I have no wish for the Duke to think that my sister is a country bumpkin!"

Ilesa felt the colour come into her cheeks.

It had always been the same whenever she was with Doreen and she was always made to feel awkward and out of place and definitely inferior.

"I will put on the best dress I have," she nodded rising to her feet. "At the same time, Doreen, as you are well aware, there has been very little money to spend on clothes. Papa has to help the people who have been unemployed ever since Uncle Robert closed up The Hall and went off to India."

"If you had any sense," Doreen retorted, "you would not allow Papa to throw his money away on a lot of ne'er-do-wells!"

She rose as well and added,

"I had better come upstairs with you and see how I can make you look at least decent!"

"I think," Ilesa said in a small voice, "we should have luncheon first. It looks as if Papa will not be back in time. It will be ready by now and Mrs. Briggs will be upset – if we let it get cold."

"Oh, very well," Doreen replied with bad grace, "and for Goodness sake see if there is something decent to eat in the house in case, although I think it is unlikely, the Duke stays for dinner."

Ilesa's eyes widened.

She knew that without any warning that this would be a catastrophe.

It was then that old Briggs, who acted as butler when required, opened the door.

He had been at the Vicarage for as long as his wife and he had, however, never been a butler in the proper sense of the word, but, because he loved his Master and his Mistress, when she had been alive, he had done his best.

Now, like Nanny and his wife, he was really one of the family.

"Luncheon be ready, Miss Ilesa," he announced, "and Mrs. Briggs says she's done her best, but she can't do no miracles at a moment's notice and that's the truth!"

Doreen did not speak and Ilesa said,

"I am sure that Mrs. Briggs has worked miracles as she always does!"

Briggs smiled at her before he hobbled rather than walked because of his rheumatism down the passage and into the dining room.

Doreen moved elegantly across the room.

"We need not waste too much time in eating when we have so much else to do," she propounded.

Ilesa did not answer. She was thinking how disappointed Mrs. Briggs would be if Doreen did not say something nice to her when luncheon was finished.

They walked into the dining room.

It was a pretty room and, as with the drawing room, the windows overlooked the garden and what had been beautifully tended flower beds.

The silver on the table shone brightly in the sunlight and, if there was one thing that Briggs enjoyed, it was cleaning the silver and he also carved the lamb as well as the Vicar might have done himself.

When he served it, Ilesa thought it so well cooked that it would be difficult for Doreen to find fault or indeed anyone else for that matter.

All the same luncheon was an uncomfortable meal with Doreen saying very little and Ilesa was feeling nervous about what was going to happen.

She was wondering, if the Duke really did arrive, as Doreen was so confident that he would, how she could leave the two of them alone without it appearing contrived.

It might turn out to be most embarrassing if the Duke guessed what was expected of him.

Ilesa knew very little about men and yet she was sure that a man like the Duke would resent being pressurised into doing anything he did not want to do.

In fact he might very well manage to avoid being put in a compromising situation.

In which case Doreen would obviously be extremely angry and complain that it was all Ilesa's fault.

When they had finished the lamb, which was delicately tender, and the new potatoes that went with it there was a dish of fresh strawberries.

Fortunately Ilesa had picked them only yesterday in the overgrown Kitchen Garden at The Hall and she knew that Mrs. Briggs had been keeping them aside as a treat for her father.

They were served at luncheon with a junket that she had made originally just for Ilesa.

Doreen refused both dishes.

"I don't like strawberries," she grumbled, "and as for junket, I have not seen it since I left the nursery!"

Because it was possible that what she said might be overheard in the kitchen, Ilesa felt embarrassed.

She gave a warning glance at her sister as she said,

"I am sure you remember that Mrs. Briggs's junket is quite different from anyone else's and we always think of it as a speciality of the Vicarage."

"Oh, very well," Doreen moaned.

She took a spoonful and looked at the junket disdainfully before she tasted it and then, because it was impossible to find fault with it, she ate quite a large helping.

Then there was coffee and afterwards the two sisters went upstairs to Ilesa's bedroom.

Without waiting for Ilesa to do so, Doreen pulled open the wardrobe door.

There were not many gowns hanging there and Ilesa knew all too well that most of them were well-worn and one or two were becoming threadbare.

"Surely you have something better than these?" Doreen asked disapprovingly.

"I-I am afraid – not," Ilesa answered. "I was going to ask Papa to give me a new gown, but there have been so – many other things – to do."

She hesitated over the last words as the truth was that her father spent all the money he had on other people.

"Then I suppose I shall have to lend you something."

Ilesa looked at her half-sister in surprise.

"I thought you had sent your carriage away?"

"I am not half-witted," Doreen answered. "I told my coachman to leave my luggage, which I had taken with me for the night, at the back door. I suppose you have somebody who can carry it upstairs?"

"I will go and tell Briggs to fetch one of the gardeners to do it," Ilesa said. "As you can see, he is too old and his rheumatism is too bad for him to carry anything heavy."

Doreen did not answer and Ilesa ran from the room and down the backstairs.

She found Briggs in the kitchen and told him what Doreen wanted.

"Are you sayin'," Mrs. Briggs asked, "that 'er Ladyship be stayin' 'ere tonight?"

"I am not sure," Ilesa answered.

It suddenly struck her that her sister would try to make the Duke take her with him to wherever he intended to go.

Doreen had not said so but she had sent her carriage away and there would be no way for her to leave the Vicarage unless the Duke conveyed her in his own carriage.

'Doreen is clever,' she told herself. 'I would – never have thought of that.'

It was some time before Doreen's very expensive leather trunk was brought up to her bedroom.

After the gardeners had set it down and left them alone, Ilesa undid the straps.

Doreen simply sat in a comfortable chair giving instructions.

"There is a gown I packed at the last minute," she said, "just in case I stayed for two nights at *The Three Feathers*. It is pale blue with a little muslin collar."

Ilesa found the gown, it was exceedingly pretty, but she thought far too grand to wear at an inn or for that matter in the country.

However Doreen condescended,

"I suppose I shall have to give it to you."

"Oh, you – cannot do that!" Ilesa cried. "I am sure you will want to keep anything – so beautiful."

"I have always thought that it did not suit me particularly well and was not really smart enough. But it is certainly an improvement on anything you possess."

"Thank you – *thank you* – very much!" Ilesa exclaimed. "It is a – lovely gown and I am – thrilled to have it."

She put it on while her sister sat in a chair criticising her appearance in every way that she could think of.

"Why can you not do your hair in a more fashionable manner?" she enquired. "The way you do it now went out at least five years ago!"

Ilesa smiled.

"There are not many people in Littlestone who know what fashion is," she said. "While the dogs and horses I spend most of my time with are not really very particular."

Doreen was not amused.

"You must think of your position," she lectured her, "for after all you are my sister."

"Yes – of course," Ilesa agreed, "but we have not seen anything of you lately."

"I am such a sensation in London," Doreen affirmed, "that I really have no time to go anywhere else!"

Then, as if she could not resist being boastful, she started to describe to Ilesa exactly what a success she really was.

She told her as well how many men had laid their hearts at her feet.

Ignorant of the Social world as Ilesa was, she realised that a great number of the men who paid Doreen such extravagant compliments were already married.

Because she read the racing newspapers, she knew that a number of Doreen's admirers were racehorse owners.

Her sister talked and carried on talking.

Ilesa tried to tell herself that she must not judge Doreen by the same standards and the same principles as her father upheld in the village of Littlestone.

'Hers is a different world,' she reflected, 'so different that I must not be stupid enough to compare the two.'

She was aware that it was only because she was in trouble that Doreen had deigned to come home.

She had known for a long time that Doreen had no affection for her family and, unless she had needed Ilesa's help for some reason, it would never have occurred to her to visit the Vicarage.

"Now be very very careful what you say," Doreen warned her when they came back to the problem of the Duke. "Convince him that I have been here for two nights and I have seen no one except for you and

Papa. We have just sat here in the evening talking over old times."

"And you really think His Grace will believe that," Ilesa asked, "if later Sir Mortimer tells him that he definitely saw you with Lord Randall at *The Three Feathers*!"

"It was very early in the morning and, although Hugo had unfortunately pulled back the curtains," Doreen said, "and Sir Mortimer was in a very agitated state. If he saw somebody who in a small way resembled me, he was obviously mistaken."

She paused for a moment before she went on,

"A naked woman with fair hair falling over her shoulders might be anyone and if I insist that I was not there and you confirm to him that I was here, why should the Duke believe Sir Mortimer?"

She sounded very confident, but Ilesa knew perceptively that she was in fact nervous and on edge.

She could understand that it had been a terrible shock for Doreen when Sir Mortimer had burst into her bedroom at the hotel.

Then when she learnt that it was only a false alarm, it had been infuriating to know that she was in the hands of a man she both disliked and distrusted.

With Ilesa looking very unlike her usual self, the two sisters walked down the stairs.

There was still no sign of the Vicar.

Doreen, determined to make absolutely certain that there was no possibility of there being any mistakes, suggested to Ilesa,

"You must tell Papa if he comes home after the Duke has arrived that I have come back to see you because I felt guilty at having been away for too long and I do *not* want the Duke or anyone else to know how long it has been."

"I am sure that Papa would not be so tactless as to reproach you in front of a stranger," Ilesa replied.

"Well, just tell him that I am thrilled to be back and that it would be a mistake for anyone in London to think that I was heartless or in any way ashamed of my family."

Ilesa did not answer and Doreen pouted in a disagreeable tone of voice,

"It is extremely annoying to think that The Hall is not open. I could have taken the Duke there and I am sure that he would have been extremely impressed by the way it looked in Grandpapa's day."

"It is very different now," Ilesa admitted with a sigh. "There is dust everywhere, soot has fallen down the chimneys and the windows are so dirty that they make the rooms dark in the daytime."

"I don't want to hear about it," Doreen retorted. "I just think it is most tiresome that Uncle Robert should

have rushed off to India as he did and left the place in such a terrible mess."

Ilesa knew that she was longing to show the Duke that her family had a large house and a big prosperous estate.

She thought privately that the Duke would hardly be impressed anyway. From all she had read about him he owned a great number of valuable possessions all over the country.

He was doubtless in consequence a very conceited man.

She felt that he would spoil the happy atmosphere of her home and it would be a great mistake for him to come here.

'He belongs to London,' she then told herself, 'with women like Doreen, who are very beautiful, but who do things that would have shocked Mama and, in point of fact, shock me as well!'

The hours were passing and now she was aware that Doreen was tense and listening for every sound.

To Ilesa it was a considerable relief that it seemed that the Duke was not going to appear at the Vicarage after all.

But in that case Doreen would be frantic at the idea of Sir Mortimer contacting him and making trouble before she could see the Duke.

Ilesa was telling herself that it was now definitely too late for the Duke to arrive when there came the sound of a loud rat-tat on the front door.

If it had been her father, he would have walked straight in through the front door.

Since it was not her father, it must therefore be the Duke.

Doreen was clearly thinking the same and she rose from her chair to stand in front of the fireplace.

While Ilesa was changing, Doreen had spent a great deal of time rearranging her hair and powdering her face.

She indeed looked enchanting, there was no doubt about that.

Her beauty seemed to outshine the small drawing room they were in and it was obvious that she belonged to another world.

The door opened.

"His Grace the Duke of Mountheron, my Lady!" old Briggs announced in a loud and penetrating voice.

CHAPTER THREE

The Duke of Mountheron was having breakfast with his host and hostess the Marquis and Marchioness of Exford.

He and his host had been out riding around the estate since seven o'clock and he had much enjoyed the fresh morning air and exercise. He had ridden one of the Marquis's most spirited and well-bred stallions.

They were discussing what they would do in the morning when a servant came into the room with a note on a silver salver.

He offered it to the Duke, who took it with some surprise.

He immediately recognised the handwriting and read the letter swiftly.

Then he turned to the Marchioness,

"This is a letter from Lady Barker. I had no idea that her home was in this vicinity and that her father is a Vicar."

"He is indeed," the Marchioness replied "and a very charming and delightful man."

"She tells me," the Duke went on, as if he found it hard to believe, "that her father has two excellent pictures by Stubbs that she thinks I would like to see."

"They are certainly some of his best work," the Marquis confirmed, "and Mark Harle was fortunate that his father was able to leave them to him as they were not entailed like virtually everything else of his."

The Duke raised his eyebrows and the Marquis explained,

"I should have thought that you would have known that the beautiful Lady Barker's grandfather was the Earl of Harlestone and her father a younger son."

"I had no idea," the Duke admitted.

He paused reflectively before he added,

"I have met the present Earl. Has he not gone to India?"

"He has been appointed Governor of the North-West Frontier Province," the Marquis said. "While it was undoubtedly a great honour for him, it has been a major tragedy for the neighbourhood."

"Why is that?" the Duke enquired.

"Because," the Marquis replied, "Robert Harle shut up the family house and dismissed practically all the people who worked for him. All this has worried his brother, the Vicar, a great deal."

He gave a short laugh before he continued,

"He was able to talk me into taking on two of his grooms that I do not need and an extra gamekeeper!"

The Marchioness smiled.

"No one can resist the Vicar when he is pleading! I now have two young housemaids I really don't require either."

She paused for a moment to add,

"Mark Harle's second daughter, Ilesa, is the most delightful girl and she has been trying to take her mother's place in the village. She looks after women who are ill and the young who cannot find employment now that The Hall is closed."

"As bad as that?" the Duke queried.

"Worse," the Marchioness answered. "For as you well know in a small village the owner of the Big House is almost the only employer."

The Duke nodded and the Marchioness continued,

"The distress caused by Robert Harle going to India is breaking his brother's heart and also, I think, that of Mark's daughter."

The Duke looked down again at the note he held in his hand.

"Lady Barker has invited me to call and see her father's pictures on my way home."

"Then it is certainly something you should do," the Marquis agreed, "except, of course, that you will want to add them to your own collection."

"I have a feeling," the Marchioness joined in, "that the Vicar enjoys his pictures as much as His Grace enjoys his and would not part with them for a King's ransom!"

"Then I will be very tactful and will not ask him to sell them to me," the Duke smiled.

He was now feeling more curious about the Stubbs's pictures that belonged to the Vicar.

For some time he had been buying every one that came up for sale and he had, he knew, one of the best collections of Stubbs's pictures in England.

*

Later in the afternoon the Duke drove in his travelling carriage drawn by four horses towards Littlestone village.

He was somewhat surprised that Doreen Barker had always talked about her husband and his possessions but never about her family.

He thought to himself a little cynically that perhaps she was not particularly proud of being a Vicar's daughter even if he was the younger son of an Earl.

She was certainly very beautiful and her radiant beauty had indeed taken all of London by storm.

The Duke, however, was well aware that she had pursued him since they had met rather than he might have pursued her.

He had most certainly allowed himself to submit to the obvious invitation in her very expressive eyes.

He would not have been the connoisseur that he was of women if he had not appreciated the perfection of her figure and her classical features.

It would certainly be something new to see her in the country.

He was wondering what her father, being a Vicar, thought of her somewhat outrageous behaviour in London.

The Duke was well aware that he was not Doreen's first lover. Nor, he thought with a sardonic twist of his lips, that would he be her last.

At the same time she was undeniably the most beautiful woman in Mayfair and certainly the whole of London.

As the Duke walked into the drawing room after Brigg's announcement, Ilesa held her breath.

She was anxious to see this man whom her sister intended to marry and she was very feeling very sure that she would not like him.

She strongly disapproved of the way that he and her sister were behaving.

Moreover, if, as she suspected, it was the Duke's habit to have *affaires de coeur* with every beautiful woman he met, she despised him.

'It is very wrong and Doreen should be made aware of it.' she told herself severely.

Then, as she looked at the Duke, she was surprised.

He was not in the least what she had expected.

He was tall, broad-shouldered and extremely handsome and there was something quite different about him from the picture that she had formed in her mind.

As he walked into the room, she seemed to feel his strong vibrations from the moment he appeared.

Then, as the dogs jumped up excitedly and ran towards him, he bent down to pat first one spaniel and then the other.

It was an action that seemed to make him more human and even kindly.

And most certainly more understanding than the rather intimidating Nobleman of her imagination whom Doreen was determined to marry because of his title.

Her sister moved forward.

"Drogo!" she exclaimed in a soft cooing voice that Ilesa had not heard before. "How wonderful to see you. I was praying that you would have the time to come and see me before you went on to Heron Court."

"How could I ever refuse such a delightful invitation as to see your father's pictures?" the Duke replied.

Doreen was now standing very near to him and looking up at him.

Both her hands were in his and he raised one to his lips.

"Need I say that you are looking very beautiful this afternoon?" he observed.

"That is just what I want to hear," Doreen replied again in her soft voice.

The Duke looked towards Ilesa and in a different tone of voice Doreen turned to say,

"Let me introduce my sister, Ilesa."

"Doreen never told me," the Duke said, holding out his hand, "that she had a sister."

Ilesa smiled.

"I have, of course, heard about your horses, Your Grace. Are they really as fine as the newspapers say that they are?"

The Duke's eyes twinkled.

"Better!" he asserted.

"Then you are very very lucky or perhaps very clever," Ilesa remarked.

"I think that is a somewhat roundabout compliment, which I really appreciate," the Duke laughed.

The spaniels had sat down when they had started talking and now they raised their heads as if to sniff the air

They told Ilesa at once that her father had returned.

"I think that is Papa," she said quickly to Doreen.

With a warning glance Ilesa ran across the room and let herself out into the hall.

She was not mistaken. The Vicar was just coming in through the front door.

As soon as he saw his daughter, he asked,

"Who is here? That is an exceedingly fine team of horses outside in the drive!"

"They belong to the Duke of Mountheron, Papa," Ilesa replied, "but before you meet him, I want to speak to you alone for a moment."

The Vicar seemed a little taken aback, but he put his hat down on one of the chairs and walked towards his study.

Ilesa followed him and, when they were both inside the room, she closed the door.

"Now, what is all this about?" the Vicar asked her, "and why should Mountheron of all people want to see me?"

"He has come to see Doreen," Ilesa explained.

"Doreen?" the Vicar exclaimed. "Do you mean she is here?"

"She arrived unexpectedly just before luncheon," Ilesa replied, "and, Papa, it is very very important that, when you go into the drawing room' you do *not* seem surprised to see her, because she is supposed to have been here since the day before yesterday."

"I don't know what all this is about," the Vicar murmured apprehensively.

"I know it's complicated, Papa," Ilesa responded, "but please, it is absolutely vital that you should pretend that she has stayed here at the Vicarage for the last two nights."

"I just don't understand what is going on," her father said sharply, "but I am not telling lies for Doreen or for anyone else."

"It is not exactly — a question of lies," Ilesa answered him slowly.

Then she had an idea.

"You see, Papa, Doreen is in love with the Duke and she thinks and hopes that he is about to propose to her. But she does not want him to think under any circumstances that she is running after him."

To her relief the Vicar smiled.

"That is sensible of him at any rate," he remarked. "A man always likes to do his own hunting."

"I was sure that you would understand, Papa, and please treat Doreen as if you had seen her here at dinner for the last two nights. Then we can leave her to capture the Duke in her own inimitable way."

The Vicar laughed.

"She will be very clever if she can do so and I am quite certain that Mountheron has been pursued by ambitious women ever since he left school and Doreen will find it hard to lead him to the Altar."

"She longs to be a Duchess," Ilesa admitted.

"I suppose that is the ambition of a great many women except for someone like your mother and, I hope, you."

Ilesa smiled at him.

"The only thing I want, Papa, is, when I do marry, to be as happy as you and Mama were together."

"And that is what I most certainly desire for you, my dearest girl," the Vicar replied.

Ilesa saw the pain in his eyes, which was always there when he spoke of his beloved wife.

Then he said,

"Now you have told me how I am to behave, let's go and meet the Duke!"

He walked from the study and Ilesa followed him.

When they went into the drawing room, Ilesa was aware that her sister was tense and anxious of what her father might say.

The Vicar, however, was entirely at his ease.

"This is a splendid surprise," he declared as he walked towards the Duke holding out his hand. "I could not imagine when I arrived home who of all my parishioners would have the finest team of horses I have ever seen!"

The Duke laughed.

"I am glad you admire them, Vicar. They are a new acquisition of mine and have been so well broken in that it is a delight to drive them."

The Vicar walked towards the fireplace and stood with his back to it.

"I must congratulate you," he addressed the Duke, "on your big success in the Grand National. It's a pity you were pipped at the post, but your horse certainly did its best to come in second."

"That is what I thought," the Duke agreed, "and talking of horses, Vicar, I suspect your daughter has told you why I was so anxious to visit you."

The Vicar looked at him enquiringly and Ilesa knew that he thought the Duke was about to say that he wished to marry Doreen.

Instead the Duke went on,

"I have been told that you possess two splendid paintings by Stubbs. As you may know, I have a collection of Stubbs that I am exceedingly proud of."

"I have heard that," the Vicar said, "and I understand that you bought a particularly fine painting of his at Christie's last month."

"That is true," the Duke agreed, "but I am very keen to see yours."

The Vicar made a gesture with his hand.

"Then, of course, I am only too willing to show Your Grace my Stubbs's, interesting as they are, but too few to be called 'a collection'."

He walked across the room to lead the way to the door and Doreen flashed a glance at her sister.

Ilesa realised at once that she was now feeling extremely relieved. Her father had ignored her, making it quite obvious that he took her presence for granted.

The Vicar led the way back to the study where he had been a few minutes before with Ilesa.

Hanging on one wall, so that it captured the light from the window to show it at its best, was a picture.

Ilesa, of course, knew that it was surely the most controversial and unusual of Stubbs's masterpieces.

As soon as the Duke looked at it, he gave what was almost a cry of delight.

"You have the portrait of John Musters!" he exclaimed. "I have always wanted to see it."

"I really thought that it would interest you," the Vicar smiled.

Ilesa knew its story, which she had heard a hundred times from the moment her father had acquired the picture.

John Musters had been painted by Stubbs with his wife Sophia sitting on the horse and himself standing at its head.

Unfortunately a very unhappy relationship developed between them and he believed that his wife had been unfaithful to him.

He then insisted on Sophia being painted out of the picture and replaced by the Reverend Philip Story.

Stubbs had done what he intended to do by obliterating Sophia's figure and substituting Vicar Story, but he had omitted to convert the sidesaddle that Sophia had been seated on into one appropriate to a man.

The Vicar made sure that the Duke realised this and said laughingly,

"Of course it is a sensible thing for me to have a picture of the Vicar, although I cannot rival his achievement of having fourteen children!"

The Duke laughed.

"I should hope not! But he evidently shared John Muster's passion for hunting. Muster had a famous pack of hounds by all accounts."

"We have said everything that can be said about this picture," the Vicar suggested. "Now do come and look at the other one."

The second picture that the Vicar had inherited from his father was on another wall.

It portrayed a number of individual hounds arranged across the picture as if they were posed for a judge's eye of dog, bitch, dog, bitch, dog.

The Duke stood gazing at it for some time.

"This is the only known work, Vicar," he said, "in which Stubbs arranged hounds in such a manner. You are extremely lucky indeed to have it and naturally I am very envious."

"I am quite sure that there is no need for Your Grace to be," the Vicar said, "when you yourself own so many superb examples of Stubbs's work."

"Which, of course, you must come and see," the Duke said. "When can you come to stay with me at Heron Court and tell me what I don't know about my own pictures?"

The Vicar chuckled.

"I should have to be very clever to do so, but, of course, it would give me great pleasure to see not only your Stubbs's but also your outstanding racehorses."

The Duke hesitated for a moment.

And then he suggested,

"I was on my way home today, but if you could be good enough to offer me a bed for the night, we could all go to Heron Court tomorrow."

The Vicar looked surprised.

Then before he could speak, Doreen exclaimed,

"That is a wonderful idea! I would really love Papa to see Heron Court, which is the most beautiful house I have ever known."

The way she spoke made it very clear that she appreciated its owner as well.

Then, as she realised that the Duke was looking at Ilesa, she said quickly,

"I am sure it would be difficult, however, for my sister to come. She has so many duties here in the village."

"The duties of both of us as far as that is concerned," the Vicar then chimed in, "will be finished after Matins tomorrow morning. I have no Sunday Evening Service this week."

This was most certainly true. The village was so depleted since the Big House had been closed that it was possible for the villagers who were left to make up only one congregation on a Sunday.

The Vicar had therefore for the time being discontinued Evensong and only with Ilesa he read the Service in the privacy of his own study.

"In which case," the Duke said, "it will give me great pleasure to invite you and both your daughters to Heron Court."

If he was to stay the night, it meant that he would also be present for dinner.

Ilesa slipped away to tell Mrs. Briggs that they had an extra guest for dinner as well as Doreen.

Mrs. Briggs held up her hands in horror.

At the same time Ilesa knew that she was really delighted to have the opportunity of cooking for a Duke and she would be determined to do her very best.

Briggs was resting his bad legs on a stool.

"I think," Ilesa said to him, "we have a bottle of claret that his Lordship gave Papa before he went to India."

"That be right, Miss Ilesa," Briggs nodded, "and there be some white wine 'is Lordship brings down from The Hall, not as much as we'd like, but enough for 'Is Grace."

"I know I can leave it to you, Briggs," Ilesa said.

As she left the kitchen, she was well aware that her sister had no wish for her to go and stay at Heron Court.

She had seen the expression on Doreen's face when the Duke had invited them all.

It seemed just ridiculous to her that a woman as beautiful as Doreen should be jealous of anyone especially her sister.

'I must be very careful,' she told herself. 'Anyway, why should he even notice me when Doreen is looking so entrancing?'

At the same time she recognised that she herself was vividly aware of the Duke and she supposed that it was because he was so different from any man who she had ever met before.

When she had shaken hands with him earlier, she had been aware of a strange vibration that coursed through her body like some electric current.

It was a sensation that she had never felt before in her life.

'He has a strong personality,' she told herself, 'and that is what so many people lack.'

But she could not explain to herself exactly what she meant by this observation.

When she went back to the drawing room, she found herself listening to the intonations of the Duke's voice.

She found it hard not to watch him as he talked to her father.

She did not stay long, but went upstairs to find Nanny and tell her that they had two extra visitors.

Nanny had been out the whole day visiting a woman friend of hers who was ill.

She had taken with her some of the special herbal medicine that Ilesa's mother had made for people in the village to cure all ailments.

When Ilesa went up the stairs to her room, she found Nanny taking off her bonnet.

"What's all this I hears, Miss Ilesa?" she asked. "Her Ladyship's arrived unexpectedly and now the Duke of Mountheron. I can hardly believe it!"

"It's true, Nanny," Ilesa said. "Doreen came home just before luncheon, but she is very insistent that we should pretend that she arrived two days ago."

Nanny looked puzzled.

"Why should she do that, I'd like to know?" she enquired sharply.

"Because, Nanny, she wants to marry the Duke, but she does not want him to think that she is running after him."

"Which I suppose she is!" Nanny finished. "And that doesn't surprise me at all."

"Oh, please, Nanny, be very careful because otherwise Doreen will be furious with us and it's very nice to have her back at home after so long."

"I suppose she's given you that dress you're wearing," Nanny said. "You certainly looks smart for a change!"

"She has lent it to me!" Ilesa corrected Nanny, "and what do you think, Papa and I are driving with the Duke tomorrow to stay at his country house so that we can see his famous collection of Stubbs's pictures!"

Nanny stared at her for a long moment.

Then she said,

"Well, that's good news for a change, I must say! It's time you got away from the village and saw a bit of life. From all I've heard, Heron Court's the right place for seein' a bit of grandeur."

"That is what I hope to see," Ilesa laughed. "But, Nanny, I have absolutely nothing to wear as you well know."

"We'll just have to find you somethin', dearie," Nanny said confidently, "and it's a step in the right direction if her Ladyship's givin' you some of her clothes. She's not given you so much as a cotton handkerchief these last few years!"

Nanny spoke tartly.

Ilesa knew that she had never really forgiven Doreen for not attending her stepmother's funeral.

It had caused a great deal of comment in the village and Nanny had expressed her views forcibly on a number of occasions.

Doreen, being beautiful and rich, was written up in every newspaper and yet she had never made any attempt to help her father in all that he was trying to do for the villagers.

It was an issue that Ilesa had no wish to comment on at the moment. So quickly she left Nanny's bedroom and went into her own.

She knew that the first problem before they went to Heron Court was to find something to wear for dinner this evening.

She reckoned that Doreen would be very critical and she could hardly appear downstairs in the same gown that she was wearing now.

She looked in her wardrobe and gave a deep sigh.

She had been busy helping her father these last two years when he had been so unhappy and she had not really had any time to think about herself or her appearance.

She heard Nanny going into one of the guestrooms to make up a bed for Doreen and she would then do the same for the Duke. And Ilesa went to help her.

Fortunately, because Nanny was so meticulous, the rooms were clean and dusted.

Ilesa took two vases from her own room. She put one in the room that Doreen was to occupy and the other in the Duke's.

"I expect that his groom will valet him, Nanny," she said. "Poor old Briggs will never manage to do that as well as laying the table and giving the silver an extra polish."

"I'll see to that," Nanny said. "Just you go and make yourself look pretty and I'll do your hair before you goes downstairs."

"Thank you, Nanny," Ilesa answered. "Doreen has already been more than critical of my appearance and I cannot imagine what I am going to wear this evening."

"There be a gown in your mother's wardrobe as will fit you perfectly," Nanny pointed out.

Ilesa was still.

"You don't think Papa would mind my wearing Mama's clothes?"

"I doubt he'll even notice," Nanny assured her. "Men are not very perceptive when it comes to women's clothes and the gown I be thinkin' of be a very simple one."

The Vicar had refused to have anything of his wife's removed from the room they had both used. Ilesa knew that her mother's gowns were all still hanging in the wardrobe just as they had always done.

She felt strongly that she was somehow intruding on something very sacred.

Then she knew that her mother, of all people, would want her to look her best if it helped Doreen.

It would certainly seem rather strange if, while she was so smart, her sister looked like a ragbag.

Anyway there was no time to argue.

By the time Nanny had finished the rooms, Ilesa could hear her father bringing the Duke upstairs to change for dinner.

She hurried into her own room and a few seconds later Nanny came in and joined her.

She was carrying a very pretty gown that her mother had often worn when she and her husband went out to a dinner party.

It was a very pale mauve and on Ilesa it made her look like a Parma violet.

Nanny had then arranged her hair skilfully in the same way that Doreen wore hers.

When Ilesa looked at herself in the mirror, she smiled.

"I see a strange young woman, Nanny, whom I have never met before!"

"You'll do your father ever so proud," Nanny said. "I'm not sayin' more than that."

Ilesa kissed the old woman on the cheek and walked towards the door.

"You had better go and see if you can help Doreen, Nanny," she suggested. "I am sure that she is used to a lady's maid and half-a-dozen other people to help her dress."

"It's a pity she doesn't help other people herself," Nanny answered.

Ilesa smiled.

There was no use arguing with Nanny, who always liked to have the last word and she was quite certain that she would say the same thing to Doreen.

Ilesa hurried down the stairs and was tidying up the drawing room when the Duke came in.

If he looked very impressive in his day clothes, he was overpowering in evening dress.

For a moment Ilesa just stood staring at him.

And then she was aware that he was looking at her in the same way.

Quickly, because she felt that it was embarrassing to remain silent, she said,

"I hope Your Grace has found everything you want? We don't often have people to stay and Papa would be very upset if you were uncomfortable in any way."

"I have everything I could possibly want," the Duke said, "and you cannot imagine how exciting it was for me to see two pictures by Stubbs that I had always heard of but had never seen before."

"They are Papa's joy and delight," Ilesa told him. "My grandfather had some very fine pictures by other famous artists, but, of course, they now belong to my Uncle Robert."

"I have met your uncle several times," the Duke said. "I am sure that he will be a great success in India, but I understand that closing the house has presented many problems in the village."

Ilesa sighed.

"It has been terrible for Papa. Most of the people in the village worked at The Hall and they had no idea of how to find employment elsewhere. Papa has done his best to help them, but it has not been in any way easy."

"I heard this from my hosts last night."

"The Marquis has been very kind in taking on one of the gamekeepers. He is such a nice man with a wife and five children. He could not possibly support them on the small pension which was all that Papa could give him."

"Surely your uncle should have paid them?" the Duke asked.

"He did pension off a lot of the old people, but it was impossible for him to do the same for everybody. I understand from what I have heard that it is indeed very expensive being the Governor of an Indian Province."

"That is true," the Duke agreed, "but it was hardly right to leave all the difficulties that have ensued to your father."

He paused before he added,

"And to you. I hear you are doing a great deal as well."

"It is only what Mama would have done if she was still alive," Ilesa said. "And thank you, thank you very much, for asking Papa to stay at your house. It will be so good for him to get away and forget for a while all the troubles that his parishioners bring him every day however small."

She spoke in a way that showed how much they meant to her.

The Duke was thinking how extraordinary it was that anyone so young and so beautiful should be concerned about the village people.

At the same time as he had already realised, being so supremely unselfconscious about herself.

He was used to women who flirted with him with every word they spoke, with every movement of their lips and every glance in his direction.

Ilesa spoke unaffectedly and the Duke knew that she was thinking of her father and not of herself when she talked of going to stay at Heron Court.

The Vicar joined them and Ilesa informed him,

"I forgot to tell you, Papa, Mr. Craig's arm is much better. He told me to tell you that it was all due to Mama's herbs, which he said were 'like a gift from Heaven itself'."

The Vicar smiled.

"That is exceedingly good news. I was afraid that he might have to lose his hand."

"I saw it this morning before I arranged the flowers in the Church," Ilesa said, "and it is healing perfectly."

"Who is Mr. Craig?" the Duke asked.

"He is the butcher," Ilesa replied. "He was cutting up some meat when his knife slipped and he sustained the most frightful wound just above his wrist. He lost so much blood that we were afraid that he would have to lose his hand."

"And the herbs that you treated him with saved it?" the Duke enquired as if he was trying to follow the story with interest.

"They are a special concoction that Mama always used for emergencies like this. It is very difficult to persuade a doctor to come here. Sometimes they refuse to come because there is no chance of their being paid."

"So you have taken their place," the Duke observed.

"I am not nearly as good as Mama was, but I am very excited that I have done the right thing where Mr. Craig is concerned."

The Duke was about to ask her more questions when the door opened and Doreen came into the room.

She was certainly looking fantastic in a gown that must have cost more than the Vicar's annual stipend.

As she glided towards the Duke, she glittered in the light of the setting sun.

Ilesa knew that she would look really marvellous in the candlelight on the dining room table.

The Duke was watching her curiously and, she thought appreciatively.

'I am sure that he will ask her to marry him,' Ilesa thought. 'Then Doreen will really be happy.'

As the thought came to her, she remembered the other man, the man who had loved her for some time.

The man about whom Sir Mortimer Jackson intended to make trouble for her.

'Can Doreen really love two men at the same time?' Ilesa wondered again.

Then, as she saw her sister gaze at the Duke in a very flirtatious manner, she reminded herself that she was very young and inexperienced.

There was no point in trying to understand what was going on.

It was not her world and the world that she lived in and the kind of difficulties that faced her were very different.

They concerned ordinary people whose problem was, quite simply, how to keep alive and survive a multitude of hardships.

'That is what really matters,' she told herself, 'and, if Doreen becomes a Duchess, it is very unlikely that we shall ever see her again.'

She saw her sister touch the Duke's arm in an intimate manner that was almost a caress.

'She has won!' Ilesa told herself.

Then she could not help wondering if the Duke had any idea that there were other men in her sister's life.

And, if he did know, did he mind?

CHAPTER FOUR

The next morning Ilesa awoke early and realised that she had not gone to sleep until very late.

She knew that it was wrong of her and the memory of it embarrassed her, but she had lain awake wondering if the Duke would go into Doreen's room.

She had heard her sister telling him who slept in which rooms when they went upstairs to bed.

"Papa has the large room at the end," Doreen had said, "which always seems to be out of proportion to the rest of the house. But he and Mama had a kind of suite with a dressing room for him and a boudoir for Mama where she wrote her letters."

She smiled sweetly up at the Duke.

"I used to think it very big as a child, but that was before I had been in an enormous house like yours."

She made the words sound caressing and then went on,

"Now, when I come home, I don't sleep in the room where I used to as a child, but in a guest room! As you and I are both guests, our rooms are side by side."

Ilesa had hardly listened to this conversation, but when she was in bed it came back into her mind.

She had wondered why Doreen was giving the Duke what amounted to a plan of the house.

Now the answer struck her like a thunderbolt and she was deeply shocked.

It seemed to her horrifying that the Duke should come into her father's house and behave improperly with her sister.

'I must not think about it! I will *not* think about it,' she told herself many times.

But, of course, she could not banish the whole scenario from her mind and it was a long time before she finally fell asleep.

When the morning eventually came, she became excited by the idea of going to stay at Heron Court and yet in a way she wished that the invitation had not been extended to her.

'I shall be out of place there,' she told herself. 'I have nothing in common with the Duke and his smart friends like Doreen.'

However it was too late now to draw back.

Moreover she knew that her father would insist on her being one of the party.

He had arranged the night before that they should all leave immediately after Morning Service was finished

It suited the villagers for it to be early so that they could go home to cook their Sunday luncheon. That is to say if they could afford one.

It was a fairly long drive to the Duke's house and he wanted to arrive not too late in the afternoon.

"It's very fortunate," he said, "that I came from London in this large travelling carriage."

When they climbed into the vehicle, which was open, the Duke sat on the driving seat with Doreen beside him. Ilesa and her father sat behind.

And behind them was a groom perched rather perilously on the small seat on top of the luggage.

Some of the small cases, including Doreen's hatbox, were with Ilesa and her father.

Because Ilesa had no idea what to take with her, she had left it to Nanny and her battered trunk looked slightly out of place beside Doreen's very elegant luggage that was all in the same design.

It was a lovely day and the Duke drove with an expertise that Ilesa could see that her father much appreciated.

He was very careful down the twisting lanes that led out of the village and, when they reached the main road, the Duke let the horses have their heads.

They stopped for luncheon at a delightful small inn where the Duke engaged a private room for his party and they were served a meal far superior to the food that they would have been offered in the public dining room.

They set off again and now Ilesa found herself looking forward to seeing Heron Court for the first time.

She remembered reading about the house in the racing newspapers and she had seen it illustrated in a magazine that was sometimes passed on to her when her grandfather was alive.

She was sure that she had read that it had been built by the famous Robert Adam or at least re-built and restored by him.

It was said to be one of the largest and most impressive of the Palladian mansions in the whole country.

'At least I shall see it once,' she thought to herself.

She was certain from the way Doreen had behaved that she and her father would not be invited to Heron Court again, even when she became the Duchess of Mountheron.

Doreen had been markedly possessive of the Duke and she seemed to resent it even when he talked about Stubbs's pictures with the Vicar.

She looked furious if the Duke even addressed a few words to Ilesa.

Finally they drove in through some impressive wrought-iron gold-tipped gates and up a long avenue of magnificent lime trees.

Now Ilesa could understand why Doreen was so determined to marry the Duke.

Never had she imagined that a house could be so imposing or so enormous, while at the same time it was such a fitting background for the Duke himself.

The sun was shining on the panes of a multitude of windows and she thought that they flashed a welcome to their owner as he arrived.

Even as they approached, his standard was run up on the flagpole on the roof.

And a red carpet was run down a long flight of steps that led up to the front door of Heron Court.

The Duke brought his horses to a standstill and grooms came running to hold their heads.

Then he helped Doreen down from the driving seat.

She then swept up the steps without waiting for her father or Ilesa as if the place already belonged to her.

The entrance hall was to Ilesa exactly as a Palladian hall should be.

It was perfectly proportioned and in the alcoves there were endless statues of Greek Goddesses and above the huge exquisitely carved mantelpiece there hung a good number of ancient regimental flags.

They were relics, Ilesa guessed, of battles won by the Duke's illustrious ancestors, who were stubbornly protecting their country from its enemies.

He had told them at luncheon that his aunt, Lady Mavis, would be acting as his hostess for their stay at Heron Court.

"She is my youngest aunt," he had informed them, "and is unmarried, so I find it very convenient that she can stay with me whenever I have need of a chaperone!"

There was a twist to his lips as he uttered the last word.

Ilesa thought that, if he was having someone to stay with whom he was having an *affaire de coeur*, he would not want his aunt there.

She tried not to think such things as they only upset her and were decidedly foreign to her nature.

Lady Mavis was waiting for them in the very attractive salon where they were taken as soon as they had entered the house.

She was a very pretty woman of about thirty-five and it seemed rather sad that she was unmarried.

The Duke, however, had explained, when he told them that she would be at Heron Court, that years ago she had had a most unfortunate love affair.

Her fiancé had died tragically in a most dreadful accident and she had never cared for anybody else.

Lady Mavis was dressed very simply and far more appropriately than Doreen, who was wearing an elaborate gown in a bright colour that Ilesa thought was entirely out of place in the country.

She was, of course, too tactful to say so and, when she saw Lady Mavis, she knew that she had been right.

"I have brought some guests with me, Aunt Mavis," the Duke said, kissing her lightly on the cheek. "I want to introduce you to Doreen's sister, Ilesa, and her father, the Reverend Mark Harle. He is a son of the late Earl of Harlestone and owns two magnificent Stubbs pictures that rival mine!"

"I find that hard to believe," Lady Mavis replied as she kissed the Duke.

She shook hands with Doreen, saying politely,

"How nice to see you again," before she turned to Ilesa.

She took her hand and then exclaimed,

"I did not know that Lady Barker had a sister and how lovely you are!"

Ilesa blushed because the compliment was something that she had not expected.

Then Lady Mavis shook hands with the Vicar and said,

"It was good of you to come at such short notice. I am sure that my nephew wants to make you envious when you see his collection of Stubbs."

"I am afraid that indeed I shall be very envious," the Vicar replied, "however hard I try to resist breaking that particular commandment."

They laughed at that remark.

Lady Mavis then poured out the tea that was waiting for them on two large tables by the fireplace.

She sat on the sofa in front of one of the tables and on it were arrayed a silver teapot, kettle, milk and cream jugs.

They were all standing on a very fine tray, which Ilesa thought must have been made in the reign of King George III.

She had learned so much about silver from her mother, who had taught her to recognise the different periods from the silver that her grandfather had accumulated at The Hall.

The Vicar sat beside Lady Mavis and Doreen then deliberately began what appeared to be a very intimate conversation with the Duke.

This left Ilesa to her own devices and so she looked around the room appreciating the pictures, which were all by famous artists.

There were also some very fine carved gilt tables that she thought were most probably of the period of King Charles II.

She almost started when the Duke turned and said to her unexpectedly,

"I hope you are admiring this room, Miss Harle. It was my mother's favourite and she took all the pieces she liked best from other parts of the house and arranged them all in here."

"I was thinking how beautiful it is," Ilesa replied, "and I especially admire the Charles II tables."

The Duke raised his eyebrows.

"You realised that they were Charles II?"

"I thought they must be from the style of the carving and naturally the crown appears on two of them as was usual in his reign."

She thought that it was almost an insult that the Duke was surprised that she should be so knowledgeable.

She could not therefore resist saying,

"I think that the Van Dyck over the fireplace is one of the finest paintings I have ever seen of his work."

"Now you are making me determined to show you my Picture Gallery," the Duke said. "When your father has finished his tea, I suggest that we should go first to look at my Stubbs collection before we start talking about them."

"You will not have to ask Papa twice to do that!" Ilesa smiled.

The Duke suggested it to the Vicar who rose to his feet eagerly.

"I thought that you had better come and see my Stubbs collection first and get it over," the Duke suggested. "Otherwise we shall keep talking about something that you have not yet seen."

They walked from the salon and only when they were moving down the corridor did Ilesa realise that, as they were leaving the salon, Lady Mavis had asked Doreen to stay with her.

She was certain that it was something that her sister would not wish to do, but she could not refuse.

It was in point of fact a relief to be able to talk to the Duke without Doreen scowling at her from behind his back.

The Duke took them into a room where his Stubbs collection was hung.

There were certainly a great number of them and he stopped in front of one that was named *Foxhounds in a Landscape, 1762.*

"It is believed that Stubbs painted this one at Berkeley Castle," he stated.

"I have heard that story," the Vicar replied.

Then they came to one picture entitled *Provenance,* which had been commissioned, the Duke related, by the Marquis of Rockingham.

The Vicar was thrilled by the way it was painted with an engaging background of trees and a meandering river.

"The little hut on the far bank," he pointed out, "is repeated in *Mares by an Oak Tree*."

The Duke gave an exclamation as he said,

"I wondered if you would notice that! I will show you that picture when we reach the other side of the room."

Then, as they moved on, it was Ilesa who was the more excited.

The picture they were looking at was one that she had seen reproduced in a magazine and she had never thought that she would be lucky enough ever to see the original.

It was of a cheetah and its two Indian handlers accompanying it.

"Look, Papa! *Look*!" she cried excitedly. "The picture we talked about and you said you would love to own."

"I had no idea it belonged to Your Grace," the Vicar commented.

"It is a new acquisition," the Duke explained. "I have only owned it now for the last six months."

"But it is so – beautiful!" Ilesa breathed, "and I have always – longed to see a cheetah!"

She saw the Duke's lips move as if he was about to say something pertinent to her and then he seemed to change his mind and said to her instead,

"It is, in my opinion, one of Stubbs's very best paintings. His model was the cheetah presented to King George III by Sir George Piggott, who, if you remember, was Governor-General of Madras."

He was speaking to the Vicar who then said,

"I have always heard that that particular cheetah was the very first ever seen in England."

"I am certain that is true," the Duke agreed. "George III gave him into the care of his brother, the Duke of Cumberland at Windsor Forest and who kept an extensive menagerie."

The Vicar gave a short laugh.

"I have read, of course, of how the Duke of Cumberland staged an experiment in Windsor Great Park as he wished to see how cheetahs attacked their prey."

"This cheetah," the Duke said, pointing to the animal with his finger, "attacked a stag who drove him off and the cheetah then escaped into the woods."

"I read that story," the Vicar nodded. "It killed a fallow deer before it was recaptured."

"I have heard too," Ilesa interposed, "that a cheetah is very fast and looks very beautiful when it is running."

"It is," the Duke answered, "and cheetahs are the fastest animals in the world over a short distance. They have, I believe, been known to reach a speed of sixty miles an hour!"

As if he thought that they had talked enough about cheetahs, he moved to other pictures in his collection.

But Ilesa kept looking back at what she knew had been called *The Spotted Sphinx*.

There was something about the animal that she found particularly attractive and then she wondered what it would be like to own one as a pet.

They spent a long time in the Stubbs room and then they went up the stairs to dress for dinner.

The maids had unpacked Ilesa's trunk and, when they asked her what she intended to wear, she found that Nanny had packed only two evening gowns for her.

One was the pale mauve one that had belonged to her mother and which she had worn last night.

The other one that she had certainly not expected to see was her mother's Wedding gown.

It was the most beautiful of all her mother's clothes that she had owned, but it would never have occurred to Ilesa to wear it.

It had been made when crinolines were all in fashion, but did not have the whalebone underneath it and it just had a very full skirt sweeping down from a tiny waist.

The whole gown was made of shadow lace or what Ilesa was told when she was a child was 'fairy lace'. It was so fine and delicate that it seemed no more substantial than a spider's web.

However she was sure that she would look overdressed in it.

Yet, when she put it on, she saw that nothing could be more in keeping with the house. It fitted her perfectly because her figure was similar to her mother's and the soft folds of the bertha that revealed her shoulders were very flattering.

She looked very young and very lovely and as if she had just stepped out of one of the pictures that hung on the walls.

She felt, however, a little shy as she walked slowly downstairs.

It was a relief to find that there were other guests for dinner.

There were two middle-aged couples who were the Duke's neighbours and also a tall, handsome young man who was introduced to her as Lord Randall.

She realised right away that this was the man who Doreen had been involved with at *The Three Feathers*.

He seemed very pleasant and, as Ilesa shook hands with him, she knew at once that he was not the wicked villain that she had made him out to be in her mind.

She saw him looking at Doreen, who followed her a few seconds later into the salon.

Ilesa was immediately convinced that Lord Randall really loved her sister.

Yet, because she had no intention of marrying him, there was an unmistakable agony in his expression.

From the way Doreen spoke to Lord Randall, Ilesa knew that she had expected him to be there and she guessed that Doreen had engineered it to prevent Sir Mortimer Jackson from making mischief.

She could not help thinking that it was cruel of her especially when Doreen went straight to the Duke's side as soon as he came into the room.

It seemed that she was doing it to make it clear to everyone that there was an intimacy between them.

When Ilesa next found herself sitting next to Lord Randall at dinner, she talked to him about the beautiful English countryside.

She learned that he had a house in Hampshire that he was exceedingly proud of.

"It has been in my family for four generations," he told her, "but, of course, it does not compare in any way with Heron Court."

There was a distinct note of despair in his voice.

As he spoke, he glanced across the table at Doreen whose beautiful face was turned up to the Duke's.

Ilesa felt very sorry for him.

"How long have you known my sister?" she then asked Lord Randall.

"Ever since she first came to London and swept through the Social world like a meteor from the sky!" Lord Randall replied.

Ilesa did not speak and he went on,

"Her beauty stunned me the first moment I saw her. But I suppose I should have known that she is as far out of my reach as the moon."

"She is certainly – very beautiful," Ilesa agreed.

"Too beautiful for any man's peace of mind," Lord Randall nodded.

Now there was a harsh note in his voice.

Because she felt so sorry for him, Ilesa changed the subject and talked to him about horses. She was sure that he would be interested in them and hoped that for the moment, at any rate, he would forget Doreen.

Lord Randall told her that the Duke had been his best friend when they were at Eton together.

The two of them had bought and broken in many young horses and found it an absorbing hobby.

"I suppose that Drogo is one of the best riders in England," he remarked. "Of course he owns the finest horses, but he can make even an inferior animal seem exceptional."

"My father also has a great love of horses," Ilesa said, "but we cannot afford many and have to be very careful of those we do choose."

"Are you saying you are poor?" Lord Randall asked.

"Very poor," Ilesa answered, "but we were fortunate in that, when my grandfather was alive, both Papa and I could ride any of the horses in his magnificent stable."

"I always had the idea," Lord Randall commented, "that Doreen came from a wealthy family that owned a large estate!"

"That was true of my grandfather," Ilesa told him, "but my father, being the third son, is only the Vicar of the village of Littlestone. I am sure you know as well as I do that Vicars are seldom rich. They always have to put their hands in their pockets for a great number of poor people."

"That is indeed true," Lord Randall agreed.

Ilesa was thinking how typical it was of Doreen to have talked of her grandfather's house rather than her father's.

Of course, as she had married a very rich man, it would be natural for people to assume that she had always been brought up in luxury and extravagance.

When dinner was over, they moved into one of the other Reception rooms that was just as beautiful as the salon.

The middle-aged guests soon said that they must be on their way home and therefore everyone was able to retire to bed soon after eleven o'clock.

As they went upstairs, Ilesa thought that Lord Randall was looking longingly at Doreen and she knew that her sister was deliberately avoiding him.

It was in case the Duke should think that there was anything unusually familiar about the way they spoke to each other.

When Ilesa opened the door into her bedroom, Doreen followed her and she closed the door behind her.

Then she turned round to look at Ilesa and demanded sharply,

"Where did you get that gown? And why have I not seen it before?"

"Nanny packed it for me," Ilesa responded, "and surely you must recognise it as Mama's Wedding gown?"

"It's far too elaborate and overdressed!" Doreen snapped angrily.

As she herself was wearing a gown that had a large bustle and which was decorated with flowers on either side, Ilesa could only stare at her.

"I know what you are thinking," Doreen said, "but I am a married woman and can wear chiffon glittering with diamanté. But girls should not push themselves forward and certainly not be dressed like someone on the stage!"

"It was either this or one of the gowns I wear at home which are almost in rags," Ilesa protested. "I had no idea that I might be going anywhere like this. I was going to ask Papa for a new gown, but he wanted the money for someone who is sick."

"Well, don't you dare wear that dress again!" Doreen retorted. "And I saw you talking to Hugo Randall at dinner. What were you saying?"

"We were talking about you," Ilesa replied.

"I thought you might be. For Heaven's sake, be careful! If the Duke thought that Hugo and I were close friends, he might be suspicious."

Ilesa was silent for a moment.

Then she said,

"I think Lord Randall loves you very much, Doreen."

"I know that and I am fond of him too. But you do see, I must be a Duchess! I must own this enormous house and the one in Park Lane in London."

"Can owning houses really make anyone happy?" Ilesa asked. "I should have thought that it was the men who lived in them who were the most celebrated."

There was a little pause before Doreen said,

"I *am* going to marry the Duke! It is just a question of time before he actually asks me. and you be careful what you say to Hugo Randall."

She went from the room as she spoke and Ilesa heard her hurrying down the corridor towards her bedroom.

She gave a deep sigh.

She had the feeling that Doreen was not going to be happy and, although she would never admit it, she was making a mistake.

Then she asked herself who was she to judge.

'Nobody has ever proposed to me,' she mused. 'And no one is likely to as I never meet any gentlemen in Littlestone.'

She undressed and climbed wearily into bed.

Before she fell asleep she tried not to think of her sister and her problems.

Instead she was seeing Stubbs's painting of a cheetah *The Spotted Sphinx* with the Indian handlers standing beside him.

*

Ilesa awoke very early as she always did at home. It must have been around five o'clock in the morning.

The sun, peeping between the curtains on the windows, was the pale gold of dawn.

Quite suddenly she thought that this was her opportunity to see the gardens and the lake and she might not be able to do so before she had to return home.

Her father and the Duke had talked of going to the stables soon after breakfast and she would certainly want to go with them.

She dressed herself quickly, finding that Nanny had packed the best of her simple gowns although they would not compare in any way with anything that Doreen would be wearing.

Ilesa, however, was not in the least interested in herself, but what she could see.

She slipped down the stairs to find that the front door was already open.

There were muffled sounds of servants brushing the carpets and dusting in the nearest rooms.

She walked straight out into the sunshine, thinking just how exciting it was to be able to explore everything on her own.

The gardens were wonderful. She walked over the lawns past flowerbeds and shrubs brilliant with blossom and colour.

There was a Herb Garden, which entranced her and she thought how much her mother would have enjoyed walking round it.

Then she came to an iron gate that led out of the garden into an orchard and because it seemed so inviting, she opened the gate and walked into the orchard.

Then in front of her she saw a wire fence.

As she reached it, she wondered if it would prevent her from going any further.

Then she gave a gasp.

On the other side of the fence, lying on the ground, was a large animal.

Ilesa could hardly believe her eyes, but it was a tiger!

CHAPTER FIVE

The Duke had risen early as he usually did.

Instead of going to the stables, however, as he most often would have done, he went to his menagerie.

It was a hobby that always thrilled him and was very close to his heart.

He had learned, however, that it was a great mistake to tell people about it. They either told him that they were terrified of wild animals or else lectured him that it was cruel to keep them cooped up in cages all of the time.

He was sick and tired of hearing the same arguments over and over again.

The fact that menageries had been in existence and popular in all countries since the time of Julius Caesar did not seem to impress his critics.

He therefore had placed his menagerie well out of sight of any of his guests who might wander in the gardens.

He kept it entirely for his own enjoyment and he had long term plans to expand it year by year. This would mean his going abroad to buy the animals he particularly wanted to include in his collection.

It was just half past six as he walked out through the front door, passing two maids in mobcaps who were scrubbing the steps and who then stopped to curtsey to His Grace.

He walked through the gardens, appreciating as always their timeless beauty and then he went through a door in the Herb Garden and down into the orchard.

The fruit trees were breathtakingly lovely with swathes of pink and white blossom scenting the fresh morning air.

As he gazed at them, they reminded him of how Ilesa had looked last night at dinner and he had been stunned by her beauty when he had first seen her in the Vicarage.

But wearing a picture gown that he recognised as being out of date, she looked as if she belonged to a different era.

He was still thinking of her as he reached the enclosure of his favourite animal, a tiger called 'Rajah'.

The Duke had brought him back from India as a cub and had trained him himself.

Rajah was inclined to be fierce and he made the men who looked after him feel nervous.

They never entered his enclosure alone and, when he was fed, there was always another man standing by with a sharp-pronged weapon to hold him at bay if it became necessary.

The Duke walked to the entrance and lifted the bolt.

The menagerie was locked at night, but it was always opened at dawn so that he could go in and see the animals as early in the morning as he wished.

Then, as he closed the door of the enclosure behind him, he looked for Rajah.

Instantly he was stunned into immobility.

He could see that Rajah was lying under one of the trees in his enclosure.

But then he thought that he must be dreaming!

Rajah's head was resting in the lap of a woman sitting beside him and she was stroking the tiger's head.

For a moment he felt that he must be imagining the picture that he saw before him.

Then he became aware that the woman sitting beside Rajah and stroking him fondly was Ilesa!

The Duke did not move.

He merely called out in a very low voice,

"Rajah! *Rajah!*"

The tiger raised his head.

Then slowly, almost reluctantly, he rose to his feet and ambled towards the Duke.

As he did so, the Duke asserted in a low voice,

"Get out of the enclosure immediately, but don't make any sudden movement!"

Ilesa did not move.

She merely smiled at him.

Rajah had by now reached the Duke and then started rubbing himself against him like a cat making noises of contentment.

Then just as he had done as a cub, he rose up on his hind legs and put his front paws on the Duke's shoulders.

The Duke patted him affectionately and talked to him in a soft soothing voice.

But he was fully aware all the time that Ilesa had not obeyed him.

Again he said to her in a markedly different tone of voice from the one that he had used to the tiger,

"Do as I say!"

She shook her head.

"I am quite safe," she replied. "He knows that I love him and – he would never hurt me."

The Duke stared at her incredulously.

Then the tiger demanded his attention and he patted and caressed him again.

At last the animal went down on the ground and once more rubbed his body against the Duke's legs.

It was then that Ilesa rose to her feet and exclaimed,

"He is the most beautiful creature I have ever seen! I did not know his name, but 'Rajah' is a very fitting one for him."

She was talking as she walked slowly towards the Duke.

When she reached him, she bent down to caress the tiger, moving her hand over his head and down his back.

"How can you own anything so lovely as Rajah?" she asked. "And even more exciting than your pictures?"

The tiger next turned from the Duke to rub his head against Ilesa.

She put her arms round him and kissed the top of his head.

"You are a beautiful, beautiful boy!" she sighed, "and Rajah is most certainly the right name for you."

"I am afraid that his keepers have translated it into 'Rajee'," the Duke informed her. "They are Indian and it seems to them a more appropriate name for a tiger."

Ilesa laughed.

As she did so, the Duke said,

"Is this really happening in front of our eyes? Can you and I be talking across an animal that is supposed to be very fierce?"

"I am sure that he is fierce only because people don't understand him," Ilesa pointed out. "Of course he should be treated with respect and admired by everyone."

She turned and stretched out her hands to bring the tiger's face up to hers.

"Is that not true, Rajah?" she asked him. "You want people to admire you and think how important you are."

The Duke still felt that he must be dreaming.

Then he said,

"I have other animals to show you, if you are interested."

"Of course I am," Ilesa replied. "Why did you not tell me, Your Grace, that you owned a menagerie?"

"I always keep it a secret," he answered, "but, as you have discovered it for yourself, I would like to show you my cheetahs."

Ilesa gave a little cry.

"Cheetahs? You really do have cheetahs, Your Grace?"

"I really and truly do," the Duke answered her with a smile.

Ilesa patted Rajah's head again and the Duke did the same.

Then they walked slowly through the gate, leaving the tiger standing and watching them go.

"I have had Rajah here since he was a cub and I trained him myself," the Duke said. "But I have never before known him to allow a stranger to enter his enclosure!"

Ilesa did not answer and he asked her,

"Have you always had this incredible power over animals?"

"I have never met a tiger before," Ilesa answered, "or a cheetah for that matter, but I can manage the most obstreperous horses. I used to help my grandfather's grooms break in those that were really wild."

"I find it hard to believe that what you tell me is the truth," the Duke said. "How can you look as you do and yet ride wild horses and fondle savage tigers?"

Ilesa laughed and it was a very pretty sound.

"That is the nicest compliment I have ever had, Your Grace. But then I have not received very many!"

The Duke felt certain that this was most probably true.

He had never met anyone so unselfconscious and Ilesa talked to him in a manner that was quite different from the way other women would.

They walked round the tiger's enclosure and then came to another.

When she saw what it contained, Ilesa gave a cry of sheer joy.

Moving among the trees in a large enclosure was a cheetah as beautiful as the one in the Stubbs picture.

His coat was sleek like that of a short-haired dog with black spots that were fluffy like a cat's fur.

"This is 'Che Che', as the Indian keepers insist on calling him," the Duke said. "His wife 'Me Me' is hiding from us in the bushes as she has just produced four enchanting cubs."

"This is the most thrilling thing that has ever happened to me!" Ilesa enthused.

"The cubs were born only four days ago," the Duke said, "so I doubt if Me Me will come to speak to us. But first you must meet Che Che."

Standing up on the gate of the cheetah enclosure, he asked jokingly,

"I suppose you are not too afraid to be introduced to him?"

"That is a gratuitous insult!" Ilesa protested, smiling at the same time.

They walked into the enclosure and Che Che ran towards the Duke, welcoming him as a dog or a cat might have done.

He was purring loudly as he moved his body against the Duke's legs as Rajah had done. Then he jumped up and began to lick his face.

Finally, as the Duke caressed him, the cheetah began to nibble at his ear.

"That is the greatest compliment a cheetah can pay you," he declared in a quiet voice.

Ilesa put out her hand.

To the Duke's surprise the cheetah turned towards her and started to lick her face too.

"You are now accepted as one of the family," the Duke said, "and perhaps Me Me will let us look at her cubs."

He walked towards a clump of bushes, calling out 'Me Me! Me Me!' as he did so.

There was a short pause and then a very beautiful cheetah, a little smaller than Che Che, peeped out from under some low bushes.

She did not come any nearer, but the Duke went over to her.

As he patted and caressed her, he moved the leaves of a bush to one side so that Ilesa could see the cubs.

They were rather like silver-backed jackals with a furry spotted under-carriage and a long fluffy mane on their heads.

They were very small and sweet.

And Ilesa wanted to pick one up in her arms, but then thought that it would be a mistake until Me Me knew her better.

They stayed for some time with the cheetahs and Ilesa loved every moment of it.

Then they had to said 'goodbye' to them both and the Duke took Ilesa further to another enclosure to see his monkey cage.

It was built high enough to enclose several trees that the monkeys could climb up and in all the enclosures there were huts where the animals could shelter if it was cold in the winter.

The monkey cage was so large that Ilesa learnt that it covered over an acre of ground.

"How can you keep anything so thrilling all to yourself?" she asked him.

"There are few people and I thought that no woman would enjoy it like you," the Duke replied. "Let me show you the rest of my family, which I intend to increase year by year."

He had a hippopotamus lying in a deep pool that it refused to come out, but lay looking like some huge giant in the cool water.

There were two giraffes, one of them quite small, the other very tall.

There was also a black panther, which the Duke refused to allow Ilesa to go near.

"He has been here with me only for a few months," he warned her, "and he has already attacked two of the men who look after him. I therefore absolutely forbid you, and I mean this, Ilesa, to go into his enclosure."

Ilesa did not seem to notice that he had used her Christian name for the first time.

She looked up at him with shining eyes as she asked,

"What will happen if I disobey you?"

"Apart from the fact that the panther might spoil your beauty, I should be very angry and probably would lock you in a cage in my menagerie so that you can never escape."

Ilesa laughed.

"I would be quite happy if I could play with Rajah and Che Che every day and perhaps I will grow fur like theirs to protect me when it is cold!"

The Duke did not answer.

He was thinking that nothing could be more attractive than her golden hair, which was glittering in the sun so that it was like a halo round her small pointed face.

As they left the panther, the Duke told her,

"I am afraid that this is where my menagerie ends at the moment. But I intend to make it very much bigger and I have been wondering lately if it would be possible to include bears and even elephants."

Ilesa clapped her hands.

"But, of course, you must! Your menagerie would not be complete without an elephant. And think too how majestic you would look riding it around the estate!"

The Duke laughed.

"I had not thought of that."

"It would certainly surprise your neighbours when they come to call."

"Then they will want to see the rest of my menagerie," the Duke said, "and I want to keep it to myself."

"I need not point out that you are being very selfish, Your Grace," Ilesa answered, "and, please may I go round again later today in case I never see it again?"

"Would that be such a disaster?" the Duke asked her.

"To me it would be a catastrophe!" Ilesa replied. "So please be kind and let me enjoy every moment of your exquisite menagerie while I can."

The Duke then thought that most women would like to be with him rather than with his possessions, but he replied,

"You shall have your wish on one condition."

"What is that?" Ilesa enquired.

"That you do *not* tell your sister or anyone else that you have been here."

"I would certainly not tell Doreen," Ilesa replied. "She is terrified of animals and even dislikes my dogs."

She spoke without thinking and then thought that what she had said was unkind.

"She loves your house," she said quickly, "and I can quite understand that because it is so magnificent."

"I like to think of it as my *home*," the Duke said, as if he was correcting her.

"But naturally you think like that," Ilesa smiled "Anywhere where we have been born and where we have been very happy with our parents is home, whether it be a cottage or a mansion as spectacular as Heron Court."

"Are you saying that you really prefer the Vicarage, which I admit is very attractive, to Heron Court?"

Ilesa put her head on one side as if she was thinking.

Then she said,

"You are trying to institute an impossible comparison. The Vicarage is part of me. It is where I have been blissfully happy ever since I was a child. It is difficult to think of it apart from myself."

She paused before she continued,

"But Heron Court is undoubtedly the most majestic as well as the most beautiful house I have ever seen, so you are very very lucky, Your Grace."

The Duke laughed.

"That is a clever and well-thought-out answer! And, of course, I stand here corrected for having asked the question."

Ilesa smiled and there were dimples in her cheeks as she said,

"I think actually you were trying to catch me out because you were so surprised that I could make friends with Rajah and Che Che. Please can we see them once more before we go back to the house?"

"Of course," the Duke agreed at once.

They went back to Rajah's enclosure and he bounded towards them as if he was a child running towards his parents.

As the Duke and Ilesa made a great fuss of him, he turned from one to the other as if he wanted to express his affection for both of them.

Once, as they were both running their hands through the fur down Rajah's back, the Duke unintentionally touched Ilesa's.

Unexpectedly she suddenly felt a strange sensation sweep through her.

She looked up at him and their eyes met.

And somehow it was quite impossible to look away.

Then in a voice that seemed to come from a far distance the Duke said,

"You are a very unusual person, Ilesa. I have never met anyone at all like you before."

"I think perhaps that is because you never meet anyone ordinary," Ilesa replied. "I live in the country, but I love animals. And I am most fortunate because they love me back."

"That is not surprising."

Then, as if Rajah was annoyed that he was losing their attention, he nibbled the Duke's ear, just like Che Che had done.

They suddenly realised that they had spent a long time with the animals at the menagerie.

And, when they returned to the house, the butler informed the Duke that the Vicar and Lady Mavis had waited for a while after breakfast, but had then gone riding.

"That was sensible," the Duke commented. "Miss Harle and I will have breakfast at once and tell the grooms to bring the horses round in half an hour."

"Am I really going to be able to ride – one of your magnificent horses?" Ilesa asked him with a broad smile on her face.

"You made it very obvious to me at the Vicarage that it was what you wanted to do," the Duke replied.

"I will go and change now in case I keep you waiting. I know that is an unpardonable sin!"

She did not wait for the Duke's reply, but she heard him laughing as she ran up the stairs.

Her riding habit was old and certainly not what might have been expected at Heron Court. But, because she was in such a hurry to ride, Ilesa did not think about her appearance.

She pinned up her hair in a tidy manner as she always did when she went out hunting.

She put on her hat, which was also old, but had a pretty blue gauze veil round the crown.

It was, although she did not realise it, something that was rapidly going out of fashion, but it had been correct fifteen years ago when her mother had first purchased it.

It was certainly very becoming, the Duke thought, as she hurried back into the breakfast room with shining eyes.

He knew how excited she was at the prospect of being able to ride one of his horses.

Because she was anxious to ride, Ilesa ate her breakfast very quickly and, as the Duke put down his cup of coffee, she had finished hers.

"Come along," he urged, "the horses will be waiting for us and I am waiting to see if you are as proficient a rider as you would have me believe."

"It will be very humiliating if I am thrown at the first fence!" Ilesa admitted. "But I did not mean to boast, Your Grace"

"After what I saw this morning," the Duke responded, "you are entitled to boast as much as you wish and I would not allow anyone to contradict you."

"I may have to keep you – to that promise," Ilesa replied.

She ran down the steps outside the front door and saw the grooms holding two superb horses.

They were certainly finer than anything she had ridden from her grandfather's stable and she knew that, if her father was riding an equally fine animal, he would undoubtedly be in his element.

The Duke then lifted her into the saddle and skilfully arranged her riding skirt for her over the pommel.

Then almost before he could mount, Ilesa was riding away.

She knew at once that she was mounted on the finest horse that she had ever ridden or even imagined.

There was no need to express her excitement and delight, the Duke could see it on her face.

They had now ridden onto some level ground on the other side of the Park when, without really arranging to do so, they were racing each other.

The horses obviously realised what was expected of them.

When the Duke and Ilesa reached the end of a very long field, they were running neck and neck. It would have been impossible to say who was ahead.

As they drew in their horses, Ilesa exclaimed,

"That was the most exciting ride that I have ever had. Oh, thank you! *Thank you*, Your Grace. It is a joy that I will remember for the rest of my life."

"I hope," the Duke then said quietly, "that it is something we will do very often."

She thought that he was reassuring her that she would be invited again to Heron Court when he married Doreen.

She told herself, however, that it was a privilege that she could not really count on.

She was quite certain that, once Doreen had become a Duchess she would, as she had done before, forget about her family altogether.

She would certainly not invite her father or her to Heron Court.

They rode on to the paddock near the stables and their horses flew over the jumps as if they were birds.

When finally they turned to go back to the house, Ilesa enthused,

"Thank you, thank you again! There are no words for me to tell you what a wonderful morning it has been and how happy you have made me!"

"I may have played a small part in it, but your thanks should really go to Rajah and Che Che and, of course, to Skylark, who you are sitting on at the moment."

Ilesa bent forward to pat her horse's neck.

"He is perfection!" she exclaimed. "I think really that he has been ridden across the sky by one of the Gods – perhaps carrying a message to Mount Olympus."

"You don't think of yourself as a Goddess?" the Duke asked dryly.

Ilesa smiled.

"You have forgotten that I am just a country bumpkin who lives amongst the cabbages and turnips. It is only your magic wand that has transplanted me for these sublime moments into a Paradise that I did not even know existed."

"Then that is where you will have to stay," the Duke said.

As they reached the level ground, they were racing each other again.

Doreen was just coming down the stairs as they arrived rather breathless back at the house.

When she saw that the Duke was alone with her sister, there was a sudden darkness in her eyes.

It told Ilesa immediately that she was furious.

"Where have you been?" she asked sharply. "I was told that Papa and Lady Mavis waited for you at breakfast and then rode off without you."

"I was in the garden," Ilesa said lamely.

"It was my fault," the Duke intervened. "I insisted on your sister coming back to her rather late breakfast with me. Then we went riding, but somehow missed finding your father and my aunt."

Doreen did not reply, but, as they went towards the salon, she slipped her arm through the Duke's.

"There are so many things I really want you to show me, Drogo," she said in her most caressing voice. "And I shall feel very neglected if you refuse."

"You know I will not do that," the Duke said, "and, of course, there must be things that will interest your father."

As he spoke, Lord Randall came down the corridor.

"You will hardly believe it, Drogo," he said, "but I overslept and I suppose I have missed all the fun."

"All of it!" the Duke replied. "That will teach you not to drink so much at night."

Lord Randall laughed.

"I admit I am not as abstemious as you. At the same time I am regretting that I did not ride with you this morning."

"Let's make plans for what we are going to do this afternoon," the Duke suggested.

They had reached the salon by this time and the Vicar greeted the Duke,

"Good morning, Your Grace! I hope you did not mind our going ahead of you, but we expected you to catch up with us."

"I must have gone in a different direction," the Duke replied vaguely, "but now I would like you to tell me what you would like to do this afternoon."

He stopped for a moment and then went on,

"Personally I would like to show you my racehorses. The yearlings are trained here before they go to Newmarket and I think you will enjoy viewing them."

"I shall indeed," the Vicar agreed, "and Ilesa must come with us because she is very knowledgeable on breeding."

The Duke looked at her in surprise.

"*Another* talent?" he asked.

"Papa is flattering me," Ilesa answered. "I read aloud *The Racing Times* to him, so I know quite a lot about your racehorses and how they have carried off all the important prizes, giving no one else a chance."

The Duke laughed.

Ilesa was aware once again that her sister was looking at her with fury in her eyes.

"I am sure," Doreen came in now in the sweetest of tones, "that Papa will not want to be away from his beloved parishioners for long. So, if he and Ilesa are leaving tomorrow, *we* must, Drogo dear, show them everything of interest today."

She emphasised the word 'we'.

It was then that Lady Mavis said,

"I too would like to come with you to see your horses, Drogo, and I am quite certain that Lord Randall will want to as well."

"I refuse to be left out," Hugo Randall asserted. "Why do we not get your phaetons out of the store, Drogo? I will race you as we have done before and this time I intend to have the best team."

The Duke laughed.

"That is indeed a challenge! All right, it is what we will do."

They walked round the garden and then enjoyed an early luncheon.

Ilesa hurried up the stairs to put on her hat.

She gave only a passing thought to the fact that Doreen was looking as if she was going to a Royal Garden Party.

What did her looks matter when she could ride the Duke's fabulous horses and see his superb yearlings?

She came downstairs again and walked into the salon.

Only the Duke and Doreen were there.

As she entered the room, Ilesa was aware that Doreen had her arms around the Duke's neck and was pulling his head down for him to kiss her.

Ilesa stood still feeling embarrassed at having interrupted them.

Then she realised that neither of them were aware of her presence in the room.

"Not here, Doreen!" she heard the Duke saying sharply.

CHAPTER SIX

They spent the afternoon very enjoyably as planned, seeing the yearlings being trained and watching the Duke and Lord Randall winning one race each in their splendid phaetons.

When they were going upstairs to dress for dinner, Ilesa said to her father in a low voice,

"Are we leaving – tomorrow?"

The Vicar shook his head.

"No," he replied. "I had intended to do so, but plans have changed."

Ilesa looked startled and he continued,

"The Duke has asked me to help him with the alterations he is planning for his Private Chapel here at Heron Court."

Ilesa was listening to him and he went on,

"The Chapel was actually first built in Tudor times and then it was destroyed by the Puritans and reconstructed during the reign of Charles II."

"It sounds fascinating," Ilesa murmured.

"It is," the Vicar agreed, "and Adam was wise enough to leave it alone. Unfortunately early in this century some time before Queen Victoria came to the Throne, the reigning Duke enlarged the Chapel."

He gave a short laugh as added,

"As you might imagine, the additions he made were completely alien to a Chapel of the Restoration period."

"So you are going to advise him on restoring it," Ilesa commented.

"The builders are coming tomorrow afternoon to see the Duke to discuss plans for the alterations and then we can go home the following day."

Ilesa wanted to say that this news delighted her because then she would be able to be with Rajah and Che Che again.

"You must come and look at the Chapel," her father was saying. "It is one of the few Private Chapels in England still in existence where anyone can be married without having to obtain a Special Licence from the Archbishop of Canterbury."

"Like the Mayfair Chapel!" Ilesa exclaimed.

"That is right," the Vicar agreed.

Ilesa went to her bedroom thrilled that they were to stay for another whole day at Heron Court.

She had, however, a somewhat intractable problem concerning what she was to wear that evening.

The Duke had told them before they went upstairs that he had lent the ballroom to one of his cousins who was giving a party for the young.

"They are seventeen and eighteen year olds," the Duke explained, "but we old 'fuddy-duddies' can go in later and dance to the orchestra if we wish to."

He was looking at Ilesa as he spoke.

She clasped her hands together as she cried,

"Oh, that would be really wonderful! I have never been to a ball. I only remember the children's parties that I was too old for after Mama died. But it would be delightful to dance in your beautiful ballroom."

"Then I insist on your celebrating your first appearance at a ball by dancing with me."

She dropped him a mocking curtsey.

"I am honoured, Your Grace."

Then she became aware that Doreen was looking at her in a hostile fashion.

Hurriedly she joined her father who she could see was going upstairs.

Now, as she entered her bedroom, she was wondering if it would look too obvious if she wore her mother's Wedding gown again.

To her surprise, however, the housekeeper, Mrs. Field, a somewhat formidable figure in black, was in her bedroom.

"I've been hearin' that you're goin' to the party tonight, miss," she began, "and so I was just wonderin' what you'd wear."

"I was wondering the same thing," Ilesa smiled. "But I do not have very much choice."

"I realise that," the housekeeper answered, "and I thought, seein' what a picture you made last night in that pretty lace gown, whether you'd like to have another one of the same period."

Ilesa looked at her in surprise and Mrs. Field explained,

"I've got His Grace's mother's gown she wore when she was about the same age as yourself and it's the one she was painted in."

As Mrs. Field spoke, she picked it up off the bed.

Ilesa saw that it was a gown of pale pink in exactly the same style that Queen Victoria wore when she came to the throne.

It boasted a very full skirt and a bertha that revealed the shoulders and the skirt was ornamented on either side with tiny pink roses.

The satin sash that encircled the waist was fastened at the back with a large bow.

"It's lovely!" Ilesa exclaimed. "May I really wear it?"

"I think you'll find it fits and if not the seamstress can quickly alter it, so to speak. If she stitches it on you, Rosie will be waitin' to undo it when you come to bed."

"Oh, thank you, thank you!" Ilesa cried. "It's the prettiest gown I have ever seen!"

After she had enjoyed a hot bath, the maids helped her into the gown and Ilesa thought, when she looked in the mirror, that she was like someone out of a picture.

The housekeeper had asked the gardeners for some pink roses and arranged them at the back of her head.

When Ilesa finally went downstairs, she felt that she was walking on air and was a part of a Fairytale.

At the same time something the housekeeper had told her was very much in her mind.

She had asked,

"You are quite certain that His Grace will not mind my wearing something that belonged to his mother?"

"I doubt he'd remember it," Mrs. Field answered. "His Grace lost his mother when he was only ten years old. Although he was brought up by his aunts, nothing can take the place of one's own mother."

"That is very true," Ilesa agreed, "and I miss my mother every day."

"His Grace looked unhappy for years and we in the house felt real sorry for the little boy."

This story made Ilesa see the Duke in an entirely new light.

Now, as she was nearing the salon door, she was not thinking about him as important, distinguished and rather overwhelming.

Instead she saw him as a small boy, lost and sad without his beloved mother.

When Ilesa entered the room, everybody was present except for Doreen.

As she walked towards them, there was a silence as they turned to look at her.

Then the Vicar asked in a bewildered voice,

"Is this really my younger daughter?"

"It is, Papa!" Ilesa smiled. "And I have to thank His Grace's very kind housekeeper for finding me this beautiful evening gown."

"You look lovely," Lady Mavis told her, "absolutely lovely."

Lord Randall said the same thing in a rather more flamboyant manner,

The Duke said nothing and Ilesa looked at him questioningly and then she saw a strange expression in his eyes that she did not understand.

"Y-you don't – mind my – borrowing it?" she stammered anxiously.

"You not only grace my house," the Duke replied, "but you will undoubtedly be the belle of the ball this evening."

Ilesa grinned.

"I am afraid you are flattering me, Your Grace, but I only hope that it comes true."

Doreen arrived in the room a few minutes later, obviously intending to make a dramatic entrance.

Her gown was very different from the one that she had worn the night before. It was of a deep emerald green and it accentuated the whiteness of her skin, as did the large emerald necklace that she was wearing.

Both the younger men complimented her on her appearance in fairly fulsome terms.

Ilesa realised, however, that when she looked at Doreen that she was extremely angry as seemed usual for their stay with the Duke at Heron Court.

As on the previous night, there were other guests for dinner and they were fortunately announced before Doreen could express her opinion of her sister's appearance.

As the newcomers were all hunting people, they talked of their horses and of their plans for the coming Season.

The dinner passed with everyone in a very good humour.

When dinner was over and the ladies had retired leaving the gentlemen to their port and cigars, Ilesa managed to keep away from her sister.

Lady Mavis came over and said to her,

"You look lovely, my dear, and I am so delighted that you and your father can stay on for another day. I am sure that he will be of great help to my nephew in his plans for the Private Chapel."

"Papa is very knowledgeable on historic buildings as well as architecture," Ilesa agreed.

"He seems to know everything about everything!" Lady Mavis smiled. "And he rides so well too, I feel sure that you are very proud of him."

"I only wish that Papa could have a few horses as good as those of the Duke's," Ilesa said wistfully. "We have two that are growing old and I cannot see how we shall ever be able to replace them."

"I think it is really tragic," Lady Mavis replied, "that someone who is as outstanding a horseman as your father should not be able to afford the best horses."

When the gentlemen later joined the ladies, the Duke proposed,

"We must all now go to the ballroom. My cousin is expecting us and I don't think, as her guests are so young, that the orchestra will play into the early hours of the morning."

"I thought that my dancing days were over," the Vicar said, "but actually I am looking forward to waltzing in your ballroom, which I am told is as magnificent as the rest of your house, Your Grace"

"Adam certainly did his best when he designed it," the Duke remarked. "Having said that, I will leave you to judge for yourself."

To Ilesa it was the most beautiful ballroom that she had ever seen.

The white pillars were touched with golden flowers and the painted ceiling held huge crystal chandeliers hanging from it.

The polished floor seemed to invite everyone to waltz and it was, she thought, all part of her increasingly fantastic Fairytale.

Doreen was waiting expectantly for the Duke to ask her to dance after he had introduced his party to their hostess.

But he walked up to her and said,

"This counts as a 'coming out' ball for your sister and I claim the right to be her first partner this evening."

Doreen's eyes darkened.

But before she could say anything, Lord Randall put his arm round her waist and swept her onto the floor.

The orchestra was playing an inviting waltz and Ilesa felt as if she was dancing on the clouds.

The Duke was an excellent dancer and, as they swung round and round, he said,

"You are so light I feel as if you have wings on your feet."

"That is just what I was thinking myself," Ilesa answered, "and this is very very exciting for me."

Her eyes were shining and her hair glittered golden in the light of many candles.

She thought, as the Duke twirled her faster round the room, that, if she never danced with anyone again, she would never forget this glorious moment.

Nor would she ever forget the beauty of the surroundings and how handsome the Duke was.

After the Duke she danced with Lord Randall and he was charming and attentive.

Eventually the party ended with a cotillion when there were generous presents for all the young girls, who looked like flowers in their pretty ballgowns.

It was not quite midnight when Ilesa finally went to bed.

She decided that she would get up early again so that she could spend as much time as possible with Rajah and Che Che.

*

As she had taught herself to do, Ilesa awoke early a deep sleep because she was so tired after such a full and inspiring day.

The sun was just breaking in the East and was sweeping away the last of the evening stars.

The sky was clear by the time she reached the garden.

Although she longed to stand and gaze at the flowers and linger in the Herb Garden, she felt as if Rajah and Che Che were calling for her.

The joy of being with them was a privilege that she knew she would never have again.

She then ran as fast as she could through the orchard and, when she reached Rajah's enclosure, she saw him under the big tree just as he had been the day before.

She opened the gate slowly and started talking to him and it was in the very special soft tone that she always used for animals.

She sat down on the ground beside him and put her arms round his neck.

"You are so beautiful," she murmured. "I shall think about you when I go home and send you messages, which I feel somehow you will hear."

The tiger seemed to understand and he nuzzled up against her.

Then, as she stroked his fur again, she heard the lock click behind her and the Duke came into the enclosure.

"I thought I would find you here," he observed.

He walked towards her and to Ilesa's surprise Rajah did not get up to greet the Duke.

He waited until the Duke sat down on the other side of him and then he turned his head towards him.

"I came early," Ilesa told the Duke, "because I could not bear to lose any time – when I could be with Rajah and Che Che."

She gave a little sigh.

"I shall miss them both – when I go home."

"As I am sure they will miss you," the Duke commented.

"They will have – you!" Ilesa replied.

"And I shall miss you too," he answered.

There was silence.

Then, because Ilesa was aware that something was on his mind, she looked up at him.

"I was just wondering," the Duke next said quietly, "what you are going to do about *us*."

Ilesa was very still.

"I-I don't – know what – you mean," she stammered after a moment's hesitation.

"I think you do. I fell in love with you, Ilesa, the very first moment I saw you. I could not believe that anyone could be so beautiful or so unspeakably lovely."

"I – it cannot be – true," Ilesa muttered as if to herself.

"It is true," he went on, "and now I am asking you, no begging you, to marry me."

He was looking at Ilesa as he was speaking and her eyes met his.

For a moment her whole face was transformed into a radiance that was like the burning sun itself.

It was as if she was transported out of time and space into the Fairytale world that she so fervently believed in.

Then, as the Duke watched her spellbound, the radiance faded from her face.

In a voice that seemed to come from a long way away she then blurted out,

"D-Doreen! It is – Doreen you – are to – marry!"

The Duke shook his head.

"I have no intention whatever of marrying your sister or anyone else for that matter. I have never in my life asked a woman to marry me, but I cannot live without you, Ilesa, and that is the whole and absolute truth."

As he spoke, he put his arm over Rajah and along Ilesa's shoulders.

Then, she was not quite sure how it actually happened, his lips were on hers.

It was the first time that she had ever been kissed and it was everything that she had expected and much much more.

She felt as if the bright sunshine was streaking through her breasts and her whole body responded to the vibrations that she felt from the Duke.

In a way that she did not understand she was a part of him.

Then he set her free and they just sat there and looked into each other's eyes with Rajah purring softly between them.

"I-I love you," Ilesa whispered. "I did not know that it was – love – but it is – and it is – so wonderful!"

"That is all I want to know," the Duke replied. "Now, my darling, you can share Rajah and Che Che with me. I cannot believe that many people have kissed for the first time across the back of a fully grown tiger!"

Ilesa gave a tremulous little laugh.

Then once again she turned her face away from him.

"But Doreen – is longing to – marry you. She is – determined to – marry you. How can I be so – unkind and disloyal to her?"

The Duke put out his hand and gently took hers.

"I have told you, my darling Alesa, that I never intended to marry anyone and certainly not someone like Doreen."

"But – but she – thinks you – love her," Ilesa stammered.

The way she said it told the Duke without words what she was thinking.

"Listen, my precious darling, I can well understand because you are so innocent and unspoiled that you are shocked that women like your sister should have *affaires de coeur* with men when they are married or have been married to someone else."

The colour flooded into Ilesa's cheeks and she dropped her head because she could not look at him.

His fingers tightened on hers as he went on,

"You must understand that to most men women are like lovely flowers. We would be inhuman if we did not admire their beauty and enjoy their fragrance and want to possess them if only for a short while."

"But – surely – that is wrong?" Ilesa asked.

"Not if the two people concerned both know exactly what they are doing. And, if the woman is not a young girl like yourself, but is already married. Although it may seem reprehensible that she is being unfaithful to her husband."

"Papa would – say that was – very wrong," Ilesa argued.

"And he would be entirely right in thinking so," the Duke said. "But it is something that has happened since the beginning of time. What I am trying to tell you, my sweet one, is that every man has in his heart a shrine where he puts first his mother and then the first woman he really loves. Who, if he is fortunate, is his wife. He wants her to be perfect and to belong to him, and only to him."

He paused before he added,

"That is what he is searching for from the time he grows up even if he does not want to admit it. But of course, as you will understand, he has disappointments. He thinks he has found the perfect flower, the pure lily that should be put in the shrine beside his mother, only to be disillusioned."

Ilesa was listening and she thought it very touching.

From the way he spoke and the sincerity in his voice, she knew how much his mother had meant to him.

"I have searched and searched for you," the Duke carried on, "only to find out that I was mistaken each time and the flower that I picked so eagerly had faded."

His voice deepened as he said,

"Now I have found you, Ilesa, and I can hardly believe that you are real and not just a part of my imagination. And my dreams."

"I am – real!" Ilesa insisted. "But why – oh, why do you – have to be a – Duke? Why could you – not have been an – ordinary man whom I – could love – look after and make – him happy?"

The Duke thought that it was the most moving words that he had ever heard.

He was well aware that the women like Doreen who pursued him and schemed to marry him were attracted by his title far more than they were by him as a man.

Some had wept bitterly when he had left them and at the same time he could not help being cynically aware of the truth.

Their tears would not have been so bitter if he had not been a Duke as well as an ardent lover.

When he looked across Rajah at Ilesa, he recognised that she was everything that he had longed for and everything he really wanted.

Now he realised that it was something priceless that he would have to fight for.

For the first time in his life it was going to be difficult to make a woman do what he wanted.

Where Ilesa was concerned, it would be against her conscience or perhaps her soul.

He held her hand in both of his as if he was afraid that she might escape from him or suddenly disappear up into the sky.

Then he said,

"I don't want to upset or worry you, my darling, but I swear to you that I will never rest until I have made you my wife."

He smiled at her before he went on,

"Somehow we will cope with the problems together, but I will not, *cannot* lose you."

There was a pause and Ilesa stuttered in a very small voice,

"It is not only – Doreen – but since – Mama died Papa has been so – unhappy – and I know I could not – leave him all – by himself in the Vicarage – with everybody – knocking on the – door with their – problems and – he would have to – manage alone."

She drew in her breath before she added,

"It would be – cruel and – wicked for me to – do so and Mama would be very – unhappy."

"Your father can have the choice of any Parish and any Living in my gift and there are a good number of them."

Ilesa shook her head.

"He will never – leave Littlestone. The people there – rely on him to – help them and – Papa has known them ever since he was – born in the Big House – and grew up amongst them."

She turned to look at the Duke and there were tears in her eyes and they were just about to start running down her cheeks.

"H-how – how could I – go away and leave him at – this moment? Oh – please please understand."

The Duke did not speak and she said even more piteously,

"When you – kissed me – I knew that I – loved you – and I know – now that what I have been feeling ever since – I came to – Heron Court when everything we – did was so exciting and wonderful – was really *love*."

The Duke did not speak and she went on,

"How – how could I – make you happy – or be as you – want me to be – if I knew I had deserted Papa?"

The Duke passed his hand over his forehead.

"Somehow," he said confidently, "we will find a solution. I don't yet know what it is, but I will find one."

He spoke with a determination and in a voice that she had not heard before.

Then he said after a few moments,

"You have to understand, my lovely Ilesa, that I will be suffering all the agonies of the damned if I have to think for one moment that I am going to lose you."

Ilesa made a helpless little gesture.

"What – can I – do? Oh – what can I – *do*?"

The Duke rose to his feet and, walking round Rajah, he pulled her to hers.

"We are going to solve this problem together," he promised, "but for the moment no one but Rajah shall know that I love you and that you love me although not as much as you will love me when I teach you about love. My darling, my precious, my glorious little wife-to-be, you are mine and nobody shall ever take you from me!"

The words ended on a triumphant note.

Then his arms closed round Ilesa and he began kissing her fiercely, possessively and passionately until they were both breathless.

He raised his head and Ilesa hid her face against his shoulder as he breathed,

"My darling, I will be very gentle with you. I have no wish to frighten you, but please be kind to me. I need not only your love but your kindness and understanding of how much I am suffering and how afraid I am that you will go away from me."

"I feel – already – as if I – belong to you," Ilesa said in a whisper.

"You *do* belong to me," the Duke replied positively. "We are a part of each other and it is impossible for us now to be divided."

He turned her face up to his and kissed her again.

Now his kisses were gentle, as if he was wooing her into giving him her heart and soul.

Rajah clearly thought that he was being neglected and so drew attention to himself by rubbing himself against the Duke's legs.

Then he attempted to squeeze himself between Ilesa and the Duke.

Ilesa gave a shaky little laugh.

"Rajah is – jealous! He is – another one who is – trying to prevent us – from being together!"

"We will share Rajah," the Duke suggested, "and somehow, by some miracle, perhaps by prayer we will find a way out of this maze into the Heaven that you have now opened for me."

Ilesa looked up at him.

"You are – so prestigious. Are you – certain that I am – really the right woman to be – your wife?"

"You are the *only* person I have ever considered for that position," the Duke replied. "Just as my animals love and trust you, as they have never trusted anyone else but me, so my people at Heron Court and on the other estates I own need you and want you."

His arms tightened around her again as he said,

"Oh, my precious, don't let us have to wait very long."

"I don't – know what to – do," Ilesa pleaded. "I love you – I know that – I love you, but Doreen will be so – angry and Papa will be – so miserable."

Her voice broke on the last word and the Duke suggested,

"Now we will go and talk to Che Che and maybe he will tell us all that we want to know."

He was trying in his own way to speak lightly and stop her from being so unhappy.

Because he understood and because her whole being seemed to respond to him, Ilesa allowed him to lead her out of Rajah's enclosure.

They walked hand-in-hand to Che Che's.

He was waiting for them!

He sprang at the Duke in sheer delight as they entered his enclosure.

They talked to him and Me Me came from her hiding place, moving out further than she had the day before.

She even allowed both the Duke and Ilesa to pat her and peep at her cubs

"I am sure that they understand what we are – feeling," Ilesa said.

"Of course they do! They know how lonely I have been at Heron Court without someone to share them with me."

Ilesa gave a little laugh.

"Now you are inventing a sad story for yourself," she teased. "You know perfectly well – you have had party after party here, parties in London, parties at Newmarket and you have only to ask for something – for it to be yours."

"I do *not* have to explain to you," the Duke said, "that parties are one thing and being with you is something very different. We think the same, we feel the same and really, my great love, there is no need for words between us is there?"

Ilesa knew that this was true.

She was aware that she could share her thoughts with him as she had never shared them with anyone else.

For a moment they just looked at each other.

She felt as if his lips were on hers and that waves of ecstasy were passing between them.

For a moment neither of them moved.

And then the Duke said,

"Exactly! How could anybody else ever understand except for you?"

Ilesa turned away with a little sob.

"If only – you were not – a Duke," she murmured.

She spoke tragically and the Duke gave a little laugh.

"But I am! I am sorry, my darling Ilesa, but you will just have to put up with it, although I am quite prepared to admit that it is indeed rather tiresome!"

Then suddenly they were both laughing.

The Duke was thinking that he had found the one woman in the world who really wanted him for himself.

For Ilesa his title was a sheer disadvantage together with all its pomp and circumstance.

The Duke then looked at his watch.

"It feels as if we have been here for only a few minutes and I have so much more to say to you. But unless we want people to be aware of what is happening between us, I think we should return now to the house for breakfast."

"Yes – of course," Ilesa agreed.

She kissed Che Che on top of his head.

"You are a very clever cheetah," she then whispered into his ear, "and I am sure you understand exactly what is happening."

"Of course he does," the Duke said, "and so does Rajah. I am certain that they knew while I was sad and lonely here that you were somewhere out there in the world and they arranged in their own crafty little minds how I should find you."

Ilesa laughed.

"That would make a lovely story! One day you must write it down and I will illustrate it."

"That will certainly be something that our children will enjoy," the Duke smiled.

He waited to see the colour come into her cheeks and her eyes looking shy.

Then he said,

"Oh, God, how much I love you! I will go on fighting for you, Ilesa, even if it kills me!"

CHAPTER SEVEN

Ilesa and the Duke patted Che Che again and then they walked towards the gate that led out of the enclosure.

The cheetah followed them and Ilesa looked back at him.

"I think he knows that we are worried," she observed.

"I am sure he does," the Duke answered.

They closed the gate behind them and started to walk quite quickly back through the orchard.

When they reached the Herb Garden, the Duke stopped.

"I think," he suggested, "that we ought to go into the house separately."

"Of course, that is sensible," Ilesa nodded.

She thought how clever he was at thinking of everything and looked up at him with shining eyes.

"I love you," he said in a very deep voice, "and you know how much I am worrying at the moment in case you try to escape me."

"I will – not do – that," she said, "but – "

"I know. I know!" the Duke interrupted. "There is always a 'but'. But, my darling, don't keep me waiting too long."

He did not kiss her although she was hoping that he would.

Then, as he turned to stand looking down into the fountain, she hurried away.

As she walked over the lawn, she was praying that somehow by some miracle everything would resolve itself for the best.

'What can I do, Mama?' she asked in her heart. 'What can I do? I know you are thinking of me as you always do, but you will also be thinking of Papa and I cannot leave him alone in the Vicarage when he is so unhappy."

She felt as if her prayer winged its way up to Heaven and that her mother was listening.

Then, when she reached the house, instead of going round to the front door, she slipped through the French window into the salon.

When she walked into the breakfast room, she found that her father was there with Lady Mavis and Lord Randall.

"Good morning, Papa," she greeted him and then she kissed the Vicar.

"I thought you would be out riding," he commented.

"I went into the garden," Ilesa answered quickly, "and, Papa, you must look at the Herb Garden. I know just how thrilled Mama would have been if we could have had one like it at home."

The Vicar did not answer and Ilesa walked to the sideboard where there was a long array of silver dishes containing everything that she might like for breakfast.

As she was lifting up the first cover, Doreen came into the dining room.

"I got up early," she announced before anybody could say anything, "because I think that we must do something very exciting this morning as you, Papa, will be leaving tomorrow."

There was a note in her voice that told Ilesa all too obviously that Doreen was anxious to be rid of her father and herself.

She was making it quite clear that their invitation was not to be extended any longer.

As she stood at the sideboard, Lord Randall was beside her.

"Let me help you," he offered.

Then, in a voice that only Doreen should have heard, he said,

"You are looking very beautiful. Even more beautiful than you did last night."

"That makes me think that I must persuade Drogo to give a proper ball here," Doreen answered.

Lord Randall did not speak.

Ilesa, however, could see the pain in his eyes and thought that her sister again was being unnecessarily cruel.

They were all sitting at the table when the Duke came in.

"Good morning," he said heartily. "I warn you all that it is going to be very hot today so we must choose our amusements where we will not sizzle in the heat."

"I thought," Lord Randall suggested before anyone else could speak, "that we might, Drogo, organise a competition of jumping in the paddock. I have been inspecting those new fences you have put up and I think they are magnificent."

"I have taken a great deal of trouble over them," the Duke answered, "and it is certainly an idea that we might put some of the new horses at them."

"I don't like jumping," Doreen objected petulantly.

There was a short pause before the Duke said,

"But, of course, Doreen, you must be the judge and you shall give away the prizes."

"What prizes?" Doreen enquired.

"That will be a surprise," the Duke replied, "and I will think of something really exciting for the participants and, of course, the Judge as well."

Ilesa realised by the way her sister preened herself at his words that she thought that the Duke had promised something more significant than just a prize.

Then the butler came to the Duke's side.

"Good morning, Your Grace," he began, "I thought you would like to know that Hilton has just carried in the white orchids that Your Grace brought back from Singapore. They have been arranged in a bowl and I have put them in the salon on the table by the window."

"My orchids from Singapore!" the Duke exclaimed. "I was hoping that they would come into bloom soon. Tell Hilton that I am delighted to have them."

"Very good, Your Grace."

The butler withdrew and Lady Mavis said,

"They have come on quickly in the heat. I looked at them the day before yesterday and they were not yet in bloom."

"I did the same," the Duke stated. "But I want you all to see them because they are a very rare and unusual orchid and pure white."

He glanced at Ilesa as he spoke.

She knew, because she could read his thoughts that he was thinking that it was what she was to him, pure and white.

She looked down at her plate just in case she should blush and someone round the table might notice it.

She was not aware that the Duke looked away from her with difficulty.

When he had finished breakfast, he realised that, because he had come in late, everyone else had finished too.

"Now," he said, "let's go to look at the orchids. I am sure you will think, as I did when I first saw them, that they are exceptional and quite the most beautiful flower imaginable that could come from anywhere in the world."

He then opened the door.

Doreen and Ilesa walked through it and he and Lord Randall followed them.

The Vicar and Lady Mavis were a little longer rising from the breakfast table and they all walked across the hall and into the salon.

The sun was streaming into the salon and at the far end of the room Ilesa could see the flowers on a table in front of the window.

Then, as she and her sister walked towards it, Doreen suddenly gave a shriek.

It was so penetrating and so shrill that Ilesa stared at her in astonishment.

She shrieked again,

Then Ilesa was aware that Che Che had just come in through the French window and was standing staring at them.

Doreen turned round and ran towards the two men who were standing behind her.

She flung herself against Lord Randall shouting,

"Hugo! Hugo! Save me – save me!"

His arms went round her and, as she trembled against him, he said,

"I will take care of you, my darling."

Ilesa ran towards Che Che, but the Duke was looking at Doreen in the arms of Lord Randall.

Her face was hidden in his neck and his arms held her very close against his chest.

"It looks, Hugo," the Duke said quietly, "as if I should congratulate you."

"I hope so, Drogo," Lord Randall replied.

Then he picked Doreen up in his arms and carried her across the room to where an open door led into an antechamber.

Ilesa was crouching down beside Che Che with her arms around him.

As the Duke joined her, she said,

"I knew that Che Che was worried about us and that is why he has escaped from his enclosure."

The Duke drew a deep breath of relief.

"That has solved one problem for us at any rate," he said, "and Hugo will now be very happy."

Ilesa looked at him in surprise.

"You knew that he was in love – with Doreen?"

"It was only very recently that I suspected it and that he was serious about it."

"I think," Ilesa said in a low tone, "Doreen was really in love with him all the time, but she was hypnotised by the glamour of the strawberry leaves on your Coronet."

The Duke's eyes twinkled.

"I promise you, my precious," he said, "I will wear it only on very formal occasions."

Ilesa smiled, but she did not answer him,

He sensed that she was thinking about her father.

Even if Doreen no longer stood in the way of their being together, there was still the Vicar to be considered.

The Duke turned towards her and then said softly, "I love you."

*

The Vicar and Lady Mavis had been following the rest of the party into the salon when the butler stopped them.

"Excuse me, sir," he said to the Vicar, "but I do think you should look at the morning papers, which have just arrived. And they are in his Grace's study."

The way he spoke in a deep serious tone made the Vicar look at him in surprise. At the same time he did not ask him any questions.

Lady Mavis had heard what the butler had said.

As the Vicar turned and started to walk down the corridor towards the study, she went with him.

They neither of them spoke.

The Vicar opened the door and they went into the study.

He then walked straight to the velvet stool in front of the fireplace where the day's daily newspapers were always laid out neatly.

He picked up *The Morning Post* hurriedly.

As he looked first at the front page, he gave a gasp.

The headlines seemed to spring out at him forcefully,

"BRITISH SOLDIERS AMBUSHED BY TRIBESMEN.

A MASSACRE ON THE NORTH-WEST FRONTIER.

The Governor of the North-West Frontier Province, the Earl of Harlestone, and his only son shot dead.

The Vicar read the headlines and Lady Mavis standing behind him read them as well.

She put her hand on his arm as she said gently,

"I am so sorry."

"And I am sorry for my sister-in-law," the Vicar pointed out quietly. "I must, of course, get in touch with our other relations as soon as possible."

He was talking as if to himself.

Then Lady Mavis said,

"Of course you must. It will be up to you to make all the arrangements for the bodies to be brought back and buried in the family vault."

The Vicar looked at her and she said,

"You must realise that you are now the Head of the Family and The Earl of Harlestone."

She knew as she spoke that it had not struck the Vicar that this was now his position until she had pointed it out to him.

Then, looking at her closely, he drew in his breath before he said very quietly,

"Now I can beg you to do me the very great honour of being my wife."

Their eyes met and Lady Mavis gave a little cry.

"I was so afraid," she exclaimed, "that you would not – ask me."

The Vicar put out his arms and she moved closer to him.

*

In the salon one of the Indians who looked after the Duke's menagerie appeared at the window.

He was obviously out of breath having been running as fast as he could.

When he saw the Duke, he salaamed.

"Forgive, Lord Sahib," he muttered. "Che Che slip by ver-ry quick as I go in pen. I run ver-ry fast but not catch."

"He is quite safe here," the Duke replied. "And I think in fact that he was looking for me and Miss Harle."

"Che Che love you ver-ry much, Lord Sahib," the Indian answered.

As he was speaking, he clasped a collar round Che Che's neck and attached to it a leather leading rein.

"We will come to see you later," Ilesa smiled, patting Che Che as he was led away.

"You were quite right," she said to the Duke. "Che Che knew that we wanted him and he was very clever to find us."

"I believe you drew him to you by your magic," the Duke answered, "just as you have drawn me."

They had both risen to their feet.

The Duke was putting out his arms towards her when he heard someone come into the room.

As he moved to one side, he realised that it was the butler.

"What is it?" he asked.

"I thought Your Grace should know," the butler replied, "that there is bad news for His Reverence the Vicar in the morning newspapers."

"Bad news?" the Duke questioned.

"Yes, Your Grace. The Earl of Harlestone and his only son have been shot in an uprising in India."

"Good gracious!" the Duke exclaimed.

"The Vicar and her Ladyship are in the study, Your Grace."

The butler moved away.

When they were alone in the salon, Ilesa sighed,

"Oh, poor Papa. He will be so upset."

"Of course he will be," the Duke agreed. "At the same time he is now 'rich Papa'."

Ilesa looked at him and he explained to her,

"You must realise that your father is now The Earl of Harlestone!"

"Yes, I suppose so," Ilesa said in a wondering voice. "Oh, Drogo! That means he can now employ again all the people who were dismissed when Uncle Robert went off to India."

There was a sudden lilt in her voice as she spoke and the Duke wondered how many other women would be thinking of those who were unemployed rather than the difference that her father's position would now make to her.

"We must go to Papa at once," Ilesa insisted.

"Of course," the Duke nodded.

They walked from the salon and down the corridor and the Duke opened the door of the study.

As Ilesa walked in, she saw to her astonishment that her father had his arms round Lady Mavis.

For a moment she could only stare at them.

Then before she could speak the Duke said,

"We have been told, Vicar, that you have had shocking news about your brother. Equally I feel sure that no one else could take over the position he left behind in England better than yourself."

"Thank you," the Vicar re[lied quietly. "I think I should tell Your Grace that I shall be supported in this new position that you should speak by your aunt about."

He smiled at Lady Mavis as he spoke and Ilesa thought that she had not seen her father look so happy or so carefree since her mother's death.

"Do you – mean, Papa," she asked, "that Lady Mavis is – going to marry you?"

"She has done me that very great honour," the Vicar replied, "and I know how much she will help me with all the difficulties that lie ahead."

Ilesa knew exactly what he was thinking about.

There would be the restoration of the house, the people to be re-employed and the whole estate to be brought back to prosperity again.

Then the Duke took charge.

"I want to make some suggestions that I think will be to the advantage not only of his Lordship but to the rest of us."

The three people he was speaking to looked at him in surprise and he went on,

"First I would like the new Earl of Harlestone to marry me to his daughter, Ilesa, within the next few hours."

The Vicar gave a gasp, but the Duke continued,

"I think once we have left on our honeymoon, it would be very wise if my aunt and the Earl were married today as well before they return to Littlestone."

It was now Lady Mavis's turn to look astonished until the Duke explained,

"If you wait until the family and everyone else learns of Robert Harle's death, they will know that you are in mourning and that your marriage must be postponed."

He glanced at Ilesa before he added,

"I have heard all about the problems that are waiting for you and I feel that you need the support and assistance of my aunt that she would not be able to give if you were not already married. You can be married perfectly legally simply as 'Mark Harle'."

The Vicar drew in a deep breath.

"But, of course," he admitted, "you are so right. Do you agree, Mavis my dear, to your nephew's very sensible in fact brilliant suggestion?"

"But, of course I do," Lady Mavis sighed. "I want to help you. You know I want to."

Ilesa knew instinctively by the way she spoke that she was very much in love with her father.

She thought that nothing could be better. Nothing would make him happier than to have someone so kind, gentle and understanding beside him for all the trials ahead of him.

As if they had all agreed, the Duke said,

"Now I will send at once for my private Chaplain and shall we say, Vicar, that you will marry me and your daughter at precisely eleven thirty?"

Ilesa gave a little cry.

"I want to marry you. Of course I want to marry you! But have you realised that as your wife I have nothing to wear?"

The Duke gave a little laugh.

"In which case, my darling, we will start our honeymoon in Paris. I will dress you in a way that will make your beauty even more overwhelming than it is at the moment. At the same time, as I shall be a very jealous husband, I am rather sorry that I cannot insist on your wearing a yashmak!"

They all laughed and the Vicar said,

"I feel as if I am being swept off my feet by a flood tide! But I am not complaining. I am sure, Drogo, that you are right in what you have just suggested."

"Now I will put the wheels in motion," the Duke declared, "and we must drink to our happiness. But, as it is only just after breakfast, a little later in the day."

He walked out of the study as he spoke and Ilesa went to her father and kissed him.

"I am so happy for you, Papa. Now you will have enough money to do all the things you have always wanted to do and we no longer need to know that the cottages are falling down and the people in Littlestone are half-starved."

"And I know you, my dear, will be very happy," the Vicar replied. "I have the greatest admiration for Drogo and Lady Mavis has been telling me how unhappy he was when he was a little boy and lost his mother who he adored."

"I will try to make it up to him," Ilesa promised.

Both she and her father knew that it was a vow from the depth of her heart.

When she went upstairs to her bedroom to tell the maid to pack her trunk, she found that the Duke's news had already percolated through the house.

The housekeeper and two maids were already packing what clothes she had with her.

But with the exception, of course, of her mother's Wedding dress.

"Am I to wear this dress?" she asked the housekeeper.

"But, of course, miss," the elderly woman replied, "and I have the veil that Her Grace wore at her Weddin'. The tiaras have been brought up from the safe. So you can make a choice of which one you think would suit you the best."

Ilesa looked a little bewildered and the housekeeper went on,

"This be a happy day for all of us, miss. We've been hopin' that His Grace would bring home a bride who would fill his mother's place and we'd all like her."

Mrs. Field took a breath before she continued,

"I speak for myself and all the household when I tell you truthfully, miss, that you are just the bride we hoped His Grace would choose."

Ilesa was very touched and she replied,

"Thank you very much, Mrs. Field, I know that you all will try to help me and prevent – me from making mistakes. I have never lived in such a huge mansion as Heron Court before, but I want – to make it a happy home – for my husband."

She spoke a little shyly.

The old housekeeper blinked away her tears before she responded,

"And now, miss, we have to think of what you can go away in. His Grace told me he was takin' you to Paris, but you have not much to put on before you gets there."

"That is true," Ilesa said. "It would be very kind if you could again lend me something suitable for the journey."

It flashed through her mind suddenly that she might appeal to her sister.

Then she realised that they had forgotten that it was Doreen who might make difficulties.

She would certainly not be pleased at her for marrying the Duke and then, because she was so happy, Ilesa tried not to think of Doreen's disapproval and the anger in her face at her when she thought that she was getting too close to the Duke.

'I am sure she will be happy with Lord Randall,' she tried to tell herself convincingly.

But she was still feeling a little apprehensive.

Mrs. Field found several pretty gowns which, although a little out of date, were certainly very becoming and would suit her very well.

"I wish we had more time," she commented. "But His Grace has always been in a hurry ever since I've known him. Though I never expected a Weddin' with literally only a few minutes to spare!"

Ilesa laughed.

"I shall be extremely grateful for these gowns, Mrs. Field. They are certainly very much smarter than anything I possess myself."

She had in fact hardly looked at the dresses before the maid packed them into her trunk.

But it was a new one that Mrs. Field had provided for her that really caught her eye.

It was so wonderful that, after all her anxiety, she could now marry the Duke without feeling guilty and without, she hoped, hurting anyone.

Finally she was dressed in her mother's Wedding gown and her hair was arranged in the latest fashion and covered with an exquisite Brussels lace veil.

Mrs. Field asked her which of the tiaras that had been laid out on the bed she would like to wear.

She chose the smallest, it was the least overpowering and to her the most beautiful.

It represented an arrangement of flowers all crafted in diamonds.

When Ilesa looked at herself in the mirror, she knew that the Duke would approve of what she had chosen.

To him she was a flower – and she must never fade.

She knew also that he had placed her in the very special shrine that was hidden in his heart.

One minute before half past eleven Mrs. Field opened the bedroom door.

"His Grace'll be waitin' for you in the hall, miss," she said. "May God bless you and bring you both great happiness on this the most important day of your lives."

"Thank you! *Thank you*," Ilesa cried.

The maids wished her 'good luck' and curtseyed as she walked slowly along the corridor and down the great staircase to the hall.

The Duke was there waiting for her.

She thought that she had never seen him look so magnificent.

The front of his cutaway coat was ablaze with his decorations and he wore The Order of The Garter over one shoulder.

He waited until Ilesa reached the last step of the staircase.

Then he put out his hands and took hers.

"You look, my darling," he said in a low voice, "exactly as I wanted you to look. Like an angel coming down from Heaven to help, protect and guide me in this life and all our future lives to come."

Ilesa's fingers tightened on his and he went on,

"This is how I always wanted to be married. Without a crowd sniggering and giggling. With just you and me and the people we love."

"I feel I am dreaming," Ilesa sighed. "Can this really be true?"

"I will make it true later in the day when you are really my wife," the Duke replied.

He picked up a bouquet that was lying on a side table.

As she took it from him, Ilesa realised that it was composed of the white orchids that he had brought from Singapore.

She thought that they were not only a sign of his love but had also brought them both the luck that they had never expected.

If after breakfast they had not gone into the salon to look at the orchids, no one would have known that Che Che had found his way there.

And Doreen would not have been frightened by him into Hugo's outstretched arms.

It was just as if everything that had happened had been directed in some clever and preordained way from Heaven.

Ilesa then sent up a little prayer of thanks to her mother,

"Thank you, thank you, Mama, you have brought me the happiness that you had with Papa and I shall always be grateful to you for being so wonderful to me."

As they walked along the corridor, the Duke said,

"Just in case, my darling Ilesa, it might be worrying you, Doreen and Hugo have already left Heron Court."

Ilesa looked up at him in considerable surprise and he explained,

"Hugo is taking no chances! She has promised to marry him and they left for London, driving my new team so that they will get there quickly."

"That was very kind – of you," Ilesa said.

The Duke gave a little laugh.

"I would have given Hugo all my horses and half Heron Court itself to know that you were no longer concerned about your sister. She will, I am sure, be very happy with Hugo, who really adores her."

"I am so happy that – no one is now – resenting our marriage and I am so – very very lucky that I can – marry you."

"And what do you think I feel?" the Duke enquired.

He looked down at her and then added very softly,

"I will tell you what I feel later when you are really and truly mine."

As they neared the Chapel, there was the sound of organ music being played very softly.

They walked in through an impressive Gothic doorway.

Ilesa saw at once that her father, wearing a magnificent vestment, was waiting for them at the Altar.

She realised too that, in the very short time that had been available, masses of flowers had been brought into the Chapel and there were large bunches everywhere.

With the candles lit and with sunshine streaming in through the stained-glass windows the whole Chapel was very beautiful.

There was the Duke's Chaplain to assist Ilesa's father in marrying them and the only other witness was Lady Mavis, who was sitting in one of the carved pews at the front.

Ilesa felt that she had never heard her father read the Marriage Service more movingly or more meaningfully.

At the same time there was an undoubted happiness in his voice that she had missed for the last two years.

Then finally she and the Duke knelt at the Altar and he blessed them.

Ilesa thought that she could hear the angels and archangels singing and that her mother was looking down at them.

She was smiling because it was what she had always wanted for Ilesa.

'Thank you! Ilesa said in her heart. 'And thank You – God. Please help me to make Drogo happy and everyone else who I will now be concerned with."

It was a prayer that was so intense that it brought tears to her eyes.

Then, as they rose to their feet, the Duke very gently lifted her veil and threw it back over her head.

He kissed her.

It was a kiss of dedication and told her that the vows he had just taken were very sacred.

And he would keep them to the end of his life.

*

The Duke had arranged that the moment Ilesa had changed her clothes they should leave and not attend her father's marriage to Lady Mavis.

"I think they would prefer to be alone," the Duke said. "Therefore I have given orders that they should have luncheon here and then a carriage will take them to Harlestone Hall."

"You have thought of everything," Ilesa murmured.

"I have thought of you," the Duke answered, "and I want to make certain, my precious, that you think of me and only of me, so actually I am being very selfish."

Ilesa knew that this was far from the truth.

She was well aware that it was because he thought of his people, just as he thought of his horses and his animals, that everyone at Heron Court was happy.

As they drove down the drive, Ilesa said,

"I think we ought to have said 'goodbye' to Che Che and thanked him for being so clever as to reach us just when we really needed him."

"We will thank him when we come home," the Duke replied, "and I think that we should bring back from our honeymoon some additions to the menagerie."

Ilesa clasped her hands together and looked at him with shining eyes.

"What are you thinking of," she asked.

"That is something that we can discuss together. I thought when we have bought your trousseau in Paris, my yacht will be waiting for us. We could visit Cairo and perhaps go through the Suez Canal and down the Red Sea to the Gulf."

He paused to smile at her before he continued,

"There are many strange species of animals and birds in these places that I think we should have at home. But, of course, I am prepared to leave the choice to you, my sublime wife."

"Oh, Drogo, what a wonderful idea!" Ilesa cried. "It will be very – very exciting to have a menagerie that we can add to whenever we go away and where, of course, Rajah and Che Che will always be there to welcome us home."

She sounded so excited and thrilled at the idea and the Duke thought that he had never expected to share a menagerie with his wife.

No man could be as fortunate as he was.

They stayed the night in a house that the Duke owned. It was halfway between Heron Court and a quiet cove where his yacht would be waiting for them the following day.

It was a very attractive small Elizabethan house set in a garden of roses and lavender.

It had belonged, the Duke told her, before she married, to his mother's family.

"There were other good houses, several of them. But this is the one I have kept," he said. "Every time that I have stayed here by myself, I thought that one day I might bring my wife."

"Now – I am here," Ilesa murmured.

"Do you think I am not aware of that?" he asked.

There was a look in his eyes that made her feel shy.

When she went up to change for dinner, she found that there was an old housemaid to look after her.

Jeannie had known the Duke when he was a little boy and had a great deal to say about him!

"A nicer young man there 'as never been, Your Grace," she said. "We loved 'im and often talked of who 'e'd marry. We 'oped it'd be someone who really loved 'im."

Ilesa smiled and the old housemaid went on,

"You're very beautiful, Your Grace, and I knows as soon as I saw you that your beauty be not only in your face but in your heart too and that's what we were 'opin' for!"

Ilesa felt like crying because her words were so touching.

She realised at dinner exactly how much the Duke was loved by all the old people.

Although they had only been told an hour or so earlier that the Duke was coming, the dinner was superb.

The gardeners had decorated the table with white flowers and there were vases of them all over the house.

When dinner was over, Ilesa expected to go into the attractive drawing room, but the Duke said,

"It has been a long and exciting day, my darling, and I don't want you to be too tired tomorrow."

"I don't feel at all tired," Ilesa answered. "I feel as if I am dancing in the sky, which was what I felt when you danced with me for the first time."

"We will dance again when we reach Paris," the Duke promised, "but now, my precious, I want to teach you about love."

They went into their bedroom, which boasted an old-fashioned four-poster bed.

There was the scent of lavender coming from the lace-edged sheets and the fragrance of roses wafted in through the windows.

There was no one else there in the room.

The Duke closed the door.

Then he came across the room and put his arms around Ilesa.

"How can this really have happened?" he asked. "I thought I might have to wait and fight for you for years. Now thanks to the Gods and, of course, Che Che, you are already mine. *Mine, really mine!* I do not have to wait any longer."

Having finished speaking, his lips were on Ilesa's.

He kissed her very gently at first.

Then more and more passionately so that she felt as if she melted into him and was no longer herself but a part of him.

Then she felt him very gently undoing her mother's Wedding gown.

She had worn it again tonight, because he had specifically asked that she should.

"You look lovelier in it," he sighed, "than in anything I could possibly buy you in Paris. We will keep it, my darling, and you shall wear it on every anniversary so that we will never forget the wonder and joy of our Wedding Day."

As it slipped from Ilesa's shoulders and slithered down onto the floor, the Duke picked her up into his arms.

He carried her to the big four-poster bed.

He laid her down very gently on the pillows.

Then she realised that he was blowing out the candles one by one.

Next he pulled back the curtains and moonlight streamed into the room like a silver cloud.

She could see the stars twinkling overhead like diamonds in the sky.

A few seconds later he was beside her and he drew her into his arms.

She knew then that her Fairytale had not ended as she had expected, but had just begun.

It was a Fairytale so beautiful and so rapturous that she knew that she was no longer tied to the ordinary world.

She was floating in a Paradise where there were no problems and misery but only love and happiness.

"I love you," the Duke breathed in a deep voice. "I love you from the top of your golden head to the soles of your little feet. You are mine, my darling, from now until Eternity."

"I love – *you*! I love – you for – Eternity as well," Ilesa answered.

Then, as the Duke made her his, she knew that it was true.

Their love was so deep, so magical and so perfect that it would be with them not only for this life but for many lives to come.

It was Eternal and came from God.

*

Che Che stretched himself out on the soft ground beneath the bushes and Me Me nestled close to him.

All the way back from the house the Indian had scolded him in fluent Urdu for running away.

"You bad Che Che, go off quick. Lord Sahib ver-ry angry with you."

Che Che knew that Lord *Sahib* was not angry, but pleased with him and *Memsahib* loved him with all the love in the world.

He felt it in the touch of her hands and in the soft sound of her voice.

When he saw her again, he would nibble her ear.

OTHER BOOKS IN THIS SERIES

The Barbara Cartland Eternal Collection is the unique opportunity to collect all five hundred of the timeless beautiful romantic novels written by the world's most celebrated and enduring romantic author.

Named the Eternal Collection because Barbara's inspiring stories of pure love, just the same as love itself, the books will be published on the internet at the rate of four titles per month until all five hundred are available.

The Eternal Collection, classic pure romance available worldwide for all time.

www.ingramcontent.com/pod-product-compliance
Lightning Source LLC
Chambersburg PA
CBHW022112170626
46808CB00002B/707